THE PRICE

OF

FAME

NWACHI, OTUM NWACHI

DEDICATION

My Late Father, Mr. **EDWARD OTUM NWACHI,** a mentor, gentle and honest man in the true meaning of the words, taught me a new philosophy of life; '' afflict the comfortable to comfort the afflicted'' which is tactfully orchestrated in the Maxims of telling the rich the truth about Christ and His merciful work on the cross to actually showcase their nothingness without Christ and fulfillment in Christ who is their all in all.

This conviction will make them believe right and live right and the peace the world has lost for a long time before now shall naturally come into being again.

APPRECIATION

This book would not have been possible without the combined efforts, inspired ideas,, and dogged support of PROF.CHRISTIAN ONYEBUCHI CHUKWU, PROF FRANCIS OTUNTA, DR. E. C. J. DURU, DR. V.A. ABANI, , ENGR.ALAZU ELOY, HON. CHRISTOPHER OMO ISU, HON. IKORO O. ENI, HON. ELECHI KENNETH. OKO, MR. S.O. OTOBOEZE, MR. ISRAEL OKORO, SIR. LAWRENCE E. ABANI, MR. EMMANUEL OYIM CHUKWU, PASTOR ANTHONY AZUBUIKE, MR. GODWIN EGWEU, MRS. S. C. AMADI, MRS. BLESSING BROWN, AND DR. ONWUBUIKO.

Thank you all.

PREFACE

The "Price of Fame'' starts with a rhetorical question ''if a man uses an elephant to set a trap, which other animal does he want to catch''. This is assumed to be the plight of a man who fights tirelessly to achieve everything by hook or crook, but in the end, loses all; then, what has he achieved? Vanity upon vanity, all is vanity and striving after wind, according to the Holy Scripture-the Bible.

This book, to a large extent, explains to people the sacrifices that life will naturally demand of one as one struggles to be known. In such a quest, man reaps what he sows for God is not mocked, whatever a man sows that he shall reap because the aroma of every sacrifice we conduct or make here on earth must go to God and it is recorded somewhere, and one day, the records will be opened and we must be remembered for one thing. It is either we are remembered for good or for evil, depending on the content and texture of our sacrifice.

This novel, therefore, is organized in such a manner as to direct both the leaders and the led on the worthy sacrifice that life expects of them. To restore the dignity of man, which could only be achieved when we give God His rightful place in the act of governance by accepting politics as the creative mind of God on earth, the novel prays that all shall accept this faith, remain, continue to grow, live and always act as truly worthy representatives of God for all times.

However, this awareness shall make the leaders not hoodwink into the wilderness of power tussle where they obey the whim of their minds which erodes truth, peace, love, and justice. It is correctly said, where there is no peace, there is no justice; where there is no justice, there is no forgiveness; and where there is no forgiveness, society becomes a source without resources as both human and materials resources are used as weapons rather than tools for development.

And by this singular act, the led are pushed to the wall; the led fall back on violence confirming what professor Alagoa {1999} says "when a community is driven to the wall, and in a situation of crisis where they have to fight for their right, they always fall back, in the past, on whatever resources they can use". Today, violence is the resource the lead fall back on. But thank God, God is not mocked, it is no longer news that a man brags that he is the richest man in society, but what is news to us today, is that a man can happily devote everything he has to charity.

Therefore, this is a clear indication that both the exploiters and the exploited shall be rewarded according to their work or sacrifice. Those who get rich by hook or crook shall be rewarded with evil orchestrated in shameful, slow but sure death. The measure they give out to the society shall be the measure dished out back to them. For the exploited, the good news is that they shall always have a savior no matter the time that gives them fresh air.

Posterity has always shown this; and those who get rich by merit and honest means, shall be rewarded with well garnished with everything good because their deeds were good, and this shall showcase the glorious triumph of good over evil.

TABLE OF CONTENTS

CHAPTER 1
If you are filled with pride,
Then you will have no room for wisdom

It is a truth, universally acknowledged that God works in a way that human beings may not understand! And God may in his infinite wisdom do things at his convenience without consulting any human being. Although we may, for reasons best known to us, think that God is, in some cases, late to attend to our problems, to the best of our knowledge, God is never in any way late. He may only delay attending to our problems in human wisdom, but it is to suit his time that will always be the best. That is why it is said that God's time is the best. Another astonishing way of God is that he can use anything to work out miracles, which shall bring him glory and praise by humans.

Men do not fight by title or size, but by courage", exclaimed a baby boy of about seven years of age. He continued, "Although it is, to a very large extent, believed that, when one walks at or is at the corridor of power, one is expected by the virtue of one's area of calling to keep one's eyes wide open. The same applies to one's ears and mind. And, on another hand, one is also expected to develop a very large heart to tolerate the present day's happening! Oh, a maxim and the best tool systematically fashioned, and employed by the oppressors, to perpetually enslave the oppressed! Yes, the best tool ever fashioned, and tactfully used, by the exploiter on the exploited! Oh, they kept the flag flying, by teaching us that, we are advisably expected to keep our mouths shut which has gone a long way to buttress the saying that, "whatever one does on earth, one should learn how to keep one's mouth shut, for the power of life and death lies in the tongue".

The question now is, who shall save us from this mental and peripheral slavery? None! But we shall free our minds! But to achieve this, it is obvious to note that "Gethsemane should be there, to be conquered; Golgotha should be there too, to be trodden under the feet of men; and Calvary in the quest for achieving Herculean but necessary task, that is in the overall interest of entire society, there should be no need for the spirit to be weakened or fickle mindedly faint for ''men do not fight by title or size but by courage.''

 Although, the course is or can be likened, to the situation when the rats and mice discovered their problems and had a council on how to proffer long-lasting solutions to their present problem. In the end, good suggestions were made and the best was chosen, which was to bell the cat while it is asleep, so that, any time it is coming to hunt for them, the bell on it shall always alert them and they shall all run into their hiding. Yes, this must take one courageous person to start. Who must that be? And, it must be me. At this juncture, his father, Ezebuiro who has been eavesdropping on all that the baby has been saying and as what the baby was saying kept reflecting in his mind picked interest in the discussion, thinking that the baby was discussing with somebody and decided to join them.

He entered the baby's room quietly in order not to interrupt or disrupt the discussion. But unfortunately, as he entered, he discovered that the baby was all alone talking to himself. Frankly speaking, he was not surprised at all and did not want to interrupt the flow of this inspiration and thought of the baby. The baby, on his part, did not even notice the presence of anybody but was very busy talking to himself to the extent that, any other person who does not flow with him or understand him, may misinterpret this, to be total madness. Yes, it must be me, the baby kept saying. I know it is difficult to start, but the best way to start is to start. Even if I start wrongly, let get me just started and even if I am not heard today, I may be heard tomorrow. Yes, I remember that, in the rabbit race, two things are obvious, it is either you get the rabbit killed if its chi agrees or you destroy its house. Yes, "if one thinks that the yam food of a baby may not be good enough if pounded, it can be per-boiled for the baby, it is still food." Yes, a man was on his way to the farm one fateful morning and he met the ant lying down on its back with its legs and hands all up towards heaven.

The man was sincerely touched by the way or position of the ant and hopefully concluded that all was not well with the ant, because it is said that, "when you see tortoise bath in the morning hours, prepares well for the market on a market day and decides to sit back at home, when it was supposed to be at the market square, if not for any other thing, at least to meet with its co-elders, then, either the wife or child is seriously sick to a point of death or that the tortoise itself is about to die." Quietly, but passionately the man went to the ant and asked, still in a very small voice, my friend, is there any problem with you? The ant aggressively responded, were you expecting any problem or do you have one already? And the man apprehensively said, no, my friend, but the way you are lying is enough indication or signal to tell any passer-by that something is wrong with you. Please, is anything the matter with you? Tell me, I am ready to help you to the best of my ability.

The ant haphazardly and nonchalantly answered, well, my friend, nothing is practically wrong with me, but have you not heard? The man quickly and impatiently asked, heard what? O! that they said, the heavens were going to fall today and I know it will interest you to know that I am in this position to stop it from destroying anything here on earth if it eventually falls or at least to contribute my quota of efforts together with those of others who feel concerned to stop the heaven from falling at all.

At this time, the man laughed heartily and teasingly said, my good friend, do you think anyone in his right senses would in any way believe what you have just said. The ant in turn replied rather derogatorily, yes, it is only feeble and fickle-minded people like you who would not know or understand the miracles joint and concerted efforts could be wrought out. Therefore, learn from me today that "men do not fight by titles or size but by courage." And so, with the little efforts of the courageous, moderated by the spirit of oneness and a strong sense of patriotism, and orchestrated in humility and honesty, problems or at worst still, wars could be tactfully waged against the mightiest and victory assured. Yes, very good, continued the baby, and as his father intentionally cleared his throat to make him know that somebody was with him, he quickly sprang up from the well-carved circle chair called Ekweke and ran to the father. He respectfully knelt before him and then greeted, good morning father; and he responded, good morning my son. Sorry, I thought you were discussing with somebody while I was in my room but I came to meet only you talking as if you were discussing with somebody.

The baby surprisingly said, o! father, do you mean I have been soliloquizing all this while disturbing people's peace. The father said, yes, my son. He still asked his father, are you sure? He said, yes my son. He continued, father, that was just my imagination as I was getting the inspiration from afar and I did not know, that my mouth was saying it out loud as to attract somebody around and if I actually did, please forgive me for disturbing your peace. The father said calmly, my son, you have no reason whatsoever to apologize over meditating on your mission here on earth because the destiny of a man is in his hands, provided, he shall eliminate his greatest enemy, fear of failure or fear itself. But father, if I may ask, why are all these things happening to me? It is because you have found favor in the sight of all the gods and ancestors of our land to restore the dignity of the people and to fulfill the high hopes of this great kingdom. Then, the baby said, I am at their mercy and services, if they found me a worthy vessel for this great mission, I am committed to this course. Yes, my son, that reminds me, I shall tell you some stories tomorrow at the cool of the evening. Yes, father, I shall be very happy to be with you to get all from you live and direct, and may the gods protect and guide us till then. And they parted happily.

That evening, when every family had finished their supper and were all out at the playground called Ogo for the night's moonlight plays, the baby boy did not go. This moonlight play is tactfully organized by the entire people of the kingdom to inculcate good moral values, customs, norms, and traditions known to the people with which the entire kingdom and people are known, and as handed down to them by their ancestors for their younger generations to make them good representatives and be of good reputes all the day long, thereby imbibing honesty, humility, transparency, moderated by harmonious co-existence, and orchestrated in love, peace, unity and oneness of purpose. In this, the informal education that was necessary for progress in nature and nurture, since men were the product of nature and nurture, was gotten; everybody was coordinated and incorporated into resourceful ventures and was very hardworking to actualize his or her purpose.

And to this effect, all men fought gallantly to fulfill their destiny. And so, as everyone was there at the playground, Ogo, the young boy was not there. The parents were very worried and wondered where he might be. They checked for him at where his mates were seated but could not find him as it was possible to know who was there and who was not there because they normally seat according to their age groups. The father, Ezebuiro then ordered his wife Ehihiandu to go back home and check whether or not he stayed back home. Ehihiandu, the wife complied immediately and, in the end, came back to the husband and reported that the baby boy was at home safe and sleeping. They were at ease and the end of the moonlight play, they went back home and still met him sleeping

Meanwhile, as the young boy was sleeping, he dreamt that he appeared at the playground, Ogo, and he saw the playground intimidating and crowded with people seated in rows. At the platform of the playground was a very high stool where the highest deity comfortably sat in White apparel which was touching the ground. A higher deity was sitting in front of the highest deity. Then, other deities are seated by the right and left-hand sides of the higher deity. That is, the whole scenario was in form of a conventional court sitting arrangement. There was something like a blackboard on which the names of each family were written. The names of each member of the family were boldly written under each family name. And, each family accordingly had a deity assigned to take good care of it and other smaller deities were assigned to individual members of the family.

This young boy was highly thrilled by this arrangement and had a keen interest in knowing what the scenario could be. And, as the highest deity noticed his vested and keen interest, he called on him in a still small voice, Nwachi, which means, son of God. And he answered, yes my lord! in a tremble. He continued, the arrangement you see here, is put in place to tell people generally and you in particular that everyone born into the world is born into the protection of a deity. If a man is born into any family in the world, he is born into first, the family deity, and afterward, a deity is assigned to take good care of him. In this circumstance, there is no way he could work against the wishes of the two deities, let alone the gods of the land, and be successful or progressive in life.

The highest deity continued, have you seen the way this scenario is organized, so shall it be when a man commits any crime against the Gods of the land known to humans as civil or against humanity known as a criminal. He shall appear before this noble and superior council, spiritual judgment. And, the deity attached to him in conjunct with the family deity shall come forth to plead for leniency on behalf of him, frankly pleading that the highest deity should temper justice with mercy. And in the end, if other deities are pacified and persuasively convinced that I should have mercy, then I shall have mercy;

but if the man's deities were unable to persuasively convince other deities and me perhaps because of the nature of the case in point, or the gravity of the offence committed, I shall without alternative visit the culprit with my wrath which, to a very great extent, shall make the rest of the culprit's stay on earth horribly miserable, the physical manifestation of the divine judgment. Although, when a man goes against the laws of humanity, the same thing is applicable but with few modifications. For instance, the gravity of an offence will determine the level of punishment that will be given to strike a balance and to display fair play, justice, equity, and harmonious co-existence among the people.

Therefore, the highest deity declares that it is advisable that, a man should live up to his glorious expectations by leading an upright life to avert the wrath of the most high. And, anything or faith outside this noble arrangement is against the ethics that established the good existence of humanity on earth and it is regarded as a subversive treasonable felony against humanity. When the young boy woke up and discovered that it was a dream, he was very worried but played cool to this and kept the dream to himself. He did not reveal it in any way, or try to tell anyone about it. Not even his closest companion, his father. At the dawn of the morning, he said his daily prayers which have been on how he could emancipate his people from their mental and peripheral slavery and serve his people better. After this, he went to his parents to perform his morning devotion to them, of which he was very fortunate to meet them already seated in the sitting room indicating that they were through with their morning prayers.

They exchanged pleasantries and the father asked him why he did not attend the previous night's moonlight play. He tactfully gave flimsy excuses very briefly without revealing his dreams. Humbly, he went about his normal morning business of tidying up the whole compound and washing of plates-

predominantly calabash and wooden trays, as it is their custom not to wash plated or sweep houses in the night to enable their night visitor, that is, their dead people and ancestral spirits as guards to eat from the leftover food of the night and some crumbs that may have fallen from the trays as they come to do their night watching over them.

No sooner had he finished his duties than he ran back to his parents to know the family's line of activities that morning. The parents gladly told him that, they were going to the farm to do some staking of yams. He got ready for all that was necessary for the exercise. And as he was very busy doing his part, the father was also busy sharpening his matchet, and the mother on her part was warming the food and, in the end, they were all set to move. He, Nwachi carried the staking rope called "Ehoro", the father, Ezebuiro, in turn, balanced the razor-sharp cutlass on his waist and carried a keg of drinking water, and the mother, Ehihiandu, on her part carried a wooden bowl called,

"Abo Ubi", containing the family's food, her hoe, and other farm implements. He led the way, followed by the mother, and finally, the father followed at the back. In a couple of hours, they got to the farm and after dressing up with farm clothes, work commenced in earnest, each doing one piece of work or the other. The mother was doing some weeding and the father was doing some staking while the boy was rendering some assistance. In the end, they went home, took their bath and the mother served them food and they ate happily together. However, as the mother went to see her friend Mgbechi, the wife of Olaka at the permission of her husband, the boy, and his father were at the reception hall taking fresh air.

CHAPTER 2
If you close your eyes to facts,
you will learn through accidents.

However, as this was going on, he reminded his father, Ezebuiro, of the story he promised to tell him at the cool of the previous evening. Then Ezebuiro, his father had a flashback of the events that happened when he was still very tender in age. Although, he was very small, still remembered them because, they were too memorable to be forgotten even in the next one thousand years to come. He told him plainly, although garnished with some elements of pride, that, before the advent of the white men, their kingdom was a very war-like but peaceful society and was highly rated, respected, and feared by all other kingdoms known to them. Every other kingdom was paying homage to them as they were regarded as the strongest and mightiest of all other kingdoms put together. The kingdom was not only looked upon as a mother kingdom but also as the most powerful to reckon with, and as the last resort. Other kingdoms looked up to them for assistance in times of trouble.

And so, every other kingdom was always happy to identify with them in all ways. Also mentioning the name of the village, in turn, exerts some reasonable influence in even, shaping the traditional and ethical behavior and cultural heritage of most kingdoms around them. The kingdom though relatively larger now than before lived happily on very cultural values and sanctity. This sanctity of the community was a moral police and conscience activator that helped to maintain sanity in the cultural ecosystem of the people. They had no war outside the cold war during the migration age for over fifty years. They had no money, no crime, and almost no disease because their faith or belief system was attached to the gods of the land and their unity was preached all over the world. They rarely died before ninety. Their psychological belief and orientation about humanity were that, both human and community development and crime prevention was everybody's business.

They pursued community-oriented programs and self-help projects in the kingdom. The kingdom was established through the tactful co-ordination of a woman, by her seven sons who later became great warriors and warlords, by conquest and annexation. The entire kingdom made, Eze Onyemetu, its first traditional ruler who was the grandfather of the seven sons of the woman, Nwakaego, who established the kingdom and coincidently the eldest man of the kingdom. This traditional ruler reigned over the whole kingdom very well as the kingdom was very peaceful, united in all ways and the people of the kingdom were cool-headed and cooperative to the best of their ability which resulted in the huge success historically recorded by the kingdom.

The second traditional ruler come up in the person of, Ezeogo Adiana, the son of late ichie Obumnenme, who initially followed the good steps of the first traditional ruler and the kingdom continued to enjoy peace, had love for one another, respected the dignity of man, and their unity was preached to the uttermost parts of the world. But a few years later in his regime, inexplicably to anyone or rather unfortunately for him in particular and the entire kingdom at large, a strange wind blew as a result of his deviant behavior and a strange disease came up which they called leprosy. Then, their tradition, therefore, provided for how every sector or facet of the society should be attended to in such a manner that, could enhance and promote harmonious co-existence and maintain law and order to the best of their ability, and in the true sense of the word to the entire kingdom.

Such provisions of the tradition for instance was that, if anyone is afflicted with the dreaded disease, leprosy, as they believed that only the gods had the power to inflict this on a man, as punishment for a particular form of crime committed either against the gods of the land or humanity. Such a person is ostracized from the kingdom to a secluded area carefully prepared for them called Obaka. This Obaka is very close to the central yam barn and is where all victims are kept and the victim's family shall adequately be catering for the person till the day the gods shall either require the soul and take the person back home to join their ancestors to the great beyond or have mercy by miraculously healing the person. Accordingly, in the morning hours before breakfast, any family that has a leper at the camp shall bring to the playground, Ogo, enough food that is intended to be served to their respective lepers. And as a point of duty, all the slaves of the kingdom, particularly those war captive or those given to the kingdom as sacrificial lambs as a way of appeasing the wrath of its great gods, shall all gather at the same venue after getting directives from the traditional ruler's palace on how to execute their legitimate duties religiously well.

These set of people were mandated by the provisions of the tradition to be running this errand for the entire kingdom. And as a matter of fact, they were doing this happily with every amount of sincerity and honesty, moderated by devotion and meticulous zeal, as they considered this as their own noble and royal contributions to the welfare of the kingdom. And after the errand boys must have completed their assignment or duty and then reported at the playground, Ogo, the town crier shall to this effect, enter the holy temple called, Ulo Ogo, a holy temple where no woman enters and still gives birth to babies or have any baby except certain sacrifices are made on her behalf, and immediately, the sound of the great Ikoro drum shall be heard. After this, a gun called Nkuru Ali shall also be heard notifying those lepers at their camp that their breakfast was ready.

In this circumstance, when this happens the leader of the lepers as chosen by them, shall then take the lead with a bell ringing as they all match along in a single file singing, "the unclean is passing, the unclean is passing", till they get to where the food is. Then, everyone will carry his or her own having known the calabash used in serving him or her food which also bears each leper's name, and then return to their camp. By noonday when everyone is expected to have gone to his normal daily business, the same thing that was done in the morning hours shall be repeated. As people shall be returning from their daily businesses, those who have lepers at the camp shall have a stopover at the camp to pick up their calabash and return home for the evening segment of the show.

However, it was disheartening to note that, as the kingdom was still enjoying this relative peace in every way, the Whiteman's team led by a man called Allison, landed in the territory and pitched their tent at the coastal area of the kingdom called, Ozarama. This particular point later became or was called Anisin, meaning according to the people, the coast of aliens. Frankly speaking, at the sight of this unfortunate set of people, a powerful delegation was sent to find out what the mission of these "lepers" according to the people was. They called the white men core lepers because according to them, their leprosy was better imagined than experienced or seen. They have never in their lifetime seen such a most unfortunate set of people who the gods did not have any atom of mercy or sympathy in inflicting leprosy upon. They never knew or believed even for one day that such was the original colour of their skin.

The people of the kingdom never liked them for anything, and also never understood the noise they make in the name of talking to them or the way they dressed which according to them negates the traditional dressing code of the kingdom. Everything about the Whiteman was alien and repulsive to the people of the great kingdom and immediately this new development prompted a solemn assembly of all the elders, the Traditional ruler, and his council of chiefs at the palace. The aftermath of this brief but very important meeting necessitated a general meeting that included everyone in the entire kingdom both women and children; and after about three hours of serious deliberation on the issue at stake, a consensus was reached and it was agreed also that they shall drive the alien crazy lepers out of their kingdom in other not to contaminate the rest members of the kingdom.

To this effect, the traditional ruler in conjunction with his council of chiefs and the elders of the kingdom summoned all the youth, between the ages of twenty and sixty to the palace and dismissed all others who were present at the meeting. In this latter assembly, a day was chosen and time fixed when the youth as the able-bodied army of the kingdom shall go down to the camp of the whites and drive the alien lepers away from their coastal area. Very early in the morning of the chosen day and date, all the youth gathered at the palace where they met the council of chiefs in a procedural session and were ushered in by the attendants.

And after a very brief discussion, one of the eldest men in the kingdom, Hoary Ikedi, poured out palm wine in libation, blessed them, and also appointed Icha as the leader and mouthpiece of the youth delegation on that errand and they left. In a couple of hours, they were all at the white man's camp, Anisini, where the assumed leader of the illegal immigrants, Alison, seemed to welcome them. In this circumstance, the leader of the youth, Icha, openly told the white man that they were asked by the entire kingdom to leave the coast before or within 24 hours or face unpleasant consequences which must make their further stay on the coast horribly miserable.

However, the white man did not understand the strange language and thereby pleaded that they should speak in the language that they could understand. At this juncture, there was dead silence, and after some time, the leader of the youth then devised another means of communicating their message to the white man by gesticulation which he tactfully dramatized, and they understood partially and immediately complied by packing up their things, entered their boat and moved without asking any further question, perhaps, having seen that intimidating crowd of able-bodied young men who could even make the mountain move if provoked to anger. And so, they understand that any resistance would have spelt doom for them. Then, the youth went back home and reported the success of their errand. It is pertinent to note here that, at every contact with the white man, a kingdom purification or sacrifice is done exactly as when a man comes in contact with a leper.

CHAPTER 3
Any life without challenges is
A life without history.

Few days later, the white men came back and pitched their tents again at the same place. When this was discovered, the traditional ruler together with his council of chiefs, the elders, and the youth of the entire community held a council at the palace. It was unanimously agreed that these unfortunate lepers, the white men, have blatantly refused to quit their coastal area, and, that, they shall from henceforth be used as sacrificial lambs to their gods on monthly basis.

This communiqué spurred the kingdom into mobilizing the entire age grades and they were armed to the teeth for this operation. All of a sudden, the operation started in earnest and the first-age grade invaded the camp at the dawn of the day and captured a young white man and brought him shoulder high to the holy temple, Ulo Ogo, where the elders, the council of chiefs and all other age grades were happily seated, and patiently waiting for their arrival. Before six o'clock that same morning, they were happily celebrating their first victory.

This trend of the event continued, for a very long time unabated till when the white men were sent for firearms as a way of reinforcement, to beef up their security networks, and to stop the inexplicable missing of their people. But unfortunately for this great kingdom, she never knew that things were no longer the same. However, this time was the time for the age grade of the great warlord who reincarnated you, Ogbuosidike and as usual, he prepared before others, and at the fullness of time, they invaded the unfortunate lepers, white men, camp carried out their operations perfectly well and carried out their unsuspecting victim's shoulder high away from their camp.

However, before they could reach the first stream from the coastal area to the first village of the kingdom called, Onungwu, something very strange and terrible happened. The invaders never knew that the unfortunate lepers, the white men, were armed to the teeth with firearms to ward off any further attacks on them from the host kingdom. To this effect, before the invaders could step into the stream, they heard the first gunshot and the victim shouted Ogbayomakpioo, which means, "I have been bitten by a strange and deadly scorpion", and he threw the white men he was carrying into the stream and was on his heels towards the first village.

And so it happened to all the invaders, and they all returned home bleeding profusely and painstakingly reported their present and painful ordeals with the unfortunate lepers to the kingdom. The evil report caused an uproar in the kingdom.

Unfortunately, at midnight, when it is believed that the spirit of the death normally comes to claim its victim, six able-bodied young men who were actively involved in the attack gave up the ghost. To be precise, this was the first time in the history of the kingdom that, she lost six able-bodied young men at a time which cannot happen or even be imagined in the heat of a strong war. There and then, there was the serious sound of cry that rented the air, which was enough to make feeble-minded people faint. But your grandfather did not die as other people died.

At this crossroads, the father, Ezibuioro, paused for a while. He removed his Essa cap from his head where he kept his snuffbox. The boy was keenly watching him as if it was the first time he was to see snuff. The father put the snuffbox in his left palm and used his right palm to perform certain incantations. He systematically opened the snuffbox. He deepened his right forefinger into a box, took a pinch of snuff, and tactfully and carefully directed it into his nostrils which he slowly or systematically inhaled or drove inside his skull till nothing was left on his forefinger. He rested for a very short while, and he did the same thing to the left nostril.

He did this twice to the two nostrils respectively then shouted, "Ekpuo", and kept silent for some time. He gazed into a vacuum for some time; rose from where he was sitting in the reception hall called, obi, and went out to blow off the snuff. In a couple of minutes, he entered and made himself comfortably seated on his Ekwekwe chair. The son was carefully watching him, He then cleared his throat and said, yes my son, he continued, so your father was the only surviving victim that did not die instantly as other victims died.

To this effect, therefore he called a solemn assembly of the elders, the council of chiefs in conjunction with the present traditional ruler, where he openly told them that a new and strange god has entered their kingdom and to combat the strange gods, it needs or requires tact, wisdom, faithfulness and total commitment to this course, He also told the kingdom that, the battle, to the best of this knowledge, was not carnal or physical but spiritual. Therefore, he advised that they should commit this heartbreaking course to the able hands of their gods to achieve any meaningful breakthrough or success as it is believed that "at the juncture, where two roads meet, the one who knows the road better should come and take the lead".He was of the candid opinion that, from the way, his spirit kept telling him, and as it was believed that their ancestor and gods were the best leaders in a case such as this because it was unimaginable or unheard of, the sting of a scorpion could result in the victim joining his ancestors. But if a strange scorpion's sting could result in death, then it is stage-managed by some gods. He finally and conclusively called for concerted efforts and cooperation of all men towards achieving this noble objective and also emphatically advised that, it was sheer foolishness and gross stupidity for anyone to allow one's ego or position to ruin a good plan that would have been for the best interest of one's people.

But before he could round off his speech with this piece of advice, almost all the people present were in tears partly because they had lost six warlords already and the possibility of the speaker's survival was uncertain because he was still bleeding profusely and no native herb had been able to stop the bleeding.

However, at this turning point, the people lifted their voices in Unisom and shouted, "God in heaven, our gods and ancestors where are you? God of heaven are you there quietly watching all these things happening to us? Our gods and ancestors are you still alive over there watching all these things happen to us? Where have we wronged you known to us or what is our offence collectively or individually? Please vindicate us o! God for we trust in you. God, we wait upon thee, do not put us to shame. Do not allow the raging waters and flood of this unfortunate leper to sweep us away or the torrent goes over us for our help is in the name of the lord mighty in battle, who made the heavens and the earth.

To this end also, the people used the forum to plan a very befitting burial, following the tradition of the kingdom, for the fallen heroes. The day and date were chosen and fixed and to this effect, two days before the appointed date and day, your grandfather together with other few elders and one of the eldest men in the kingdom called, onikara iheugwumere, went to the king, Ezeogo Adiana, by night to hold council on how to start the purification rites and atonement for the kingdom as a sure way of getting favour from the gods to salvage their pathetic situation or condition.

The traditional ruler on his part welcomes his august visitors and also presented kola to them as the tradition demanded to the best of his ability. Precisely speaking, at the end of the entertainment, the discussion started in earnest and the aftermath of the meeting was perfectly executed. Then all preparation was religiously completed on the eve of the sixth day. Then, on the sixth day, being the red letter day for giving the fallen heroes a befitting burial, the entire kingdom intimidatingly crowded the playground in anticipation of the ceremony.

The ceremony started at exactly eight o'clock in the morning and all burial rites were strictly observed also all that it takes to have or make a befitting burial for a departed hero according to their tradition was to the best of their knowledge and ability strictly observed. And the people though mournful at first happily wined and dined till night falls. In the end, Hoary Ejimkeonye performed the libation, closing prayer, and remarks, and that marked the end of the occasion. And all of sudden, people started dispersing from the playground and happily went back to their respective homes with the high hopes that they have given their departed heroes a befitting burial according to their tradition.

Meanwhile, at this point, your grandfather refused to die irrespective of his bleeding side. According to him, he vowed not to die until practical measures are taken to avenge the course of the departed heroes and the course of changing the present state of affairs of the kingdom to its original status, so that when he goes to join his ancestors, he shall have some good tales to tell them. To this effect, he called for another solemn assembly at the traditional ruler's palace which comprised all the able-bodied men, elders, and other warlords left. But unfortunately for the entire kingdom, the traditional ruler before this time has been having a series of secret meetings with the unfortunate lepers.

The whites have promised him all that could make him rule comfortably over the people and also assured him that his children and his children's children shall continually rule the people even against their will. Emphatically, they promised him heaven and earth provided he complies with them. And as it is generally believed that "power corrupts and absolute power corrupts absolutely," he pledged his compliance, support, and loyalty to the whims and caprices of the unfortunate lepers even unto his death provided they shall stand by their promise.

In this circumstance, as they convened, the traditional ruler actually and pretentiously received them as usual, and when that was over, Ichie Ikedi presented the agenda as mandated and the floor was opened for deliberations. But it was disheartening to note that the traditional ruler who has been the senior advocate of this course started sounding strange right from the onset because he has been brainwashed by the white men. He started telling the people stories that took them so many hours to understand.

He told the people that it is generally said that "if a man is not mature enough to avenge his father's death, what happened to the father shall definitely happen to him". He told them emphatically that the battle was not physical but needed both physical and spiritual maturity of mind to undertake, and that, it may take them some time to achieve this for the course at stake. In fact, he tactfully and systematically discouraged and frustrated all the efforts the entire kingdom had intended to apply to avenge their course.

The traditional ruler in precise terms, allowed his ego, greed, selfishness, and position to ruin the good plans that would have been for his people's interest or would have done the people good in all ramifications. At this juncture, your grandfather exclaimed, "o! Why is the might falling; o! the traditional ruler has forgotten that it is when one has nothing that miracles could happen to one. Why must the traditional ruler look at us like grasshoppers and the unfortunate lepers, giants in comparison. Then, it is no longer worth living here on earth, for "it is better to be king in hell than to be a slave in heaven!" He exclaimed and the meeting ended and people parted in annoyance. None was happy about the new development. And so, two days later after the meeting, your grandfather before he breathed his last exclaimed O! OTUM, meaning, my noble and historic society who shall save you from this mess and he joined his ancestors and was given a very befitting burial that not even a traditional ruler of the kingdom has ever received.

CHAPTER 4

True freedom fighters were termed Hoodlums; the actual hoodlums were termed saints; and looters and betrayers in the name of leaders were termed God's sent.

And so, from that day and moment, the entire kingdom strived for warlords, and the traditional ruler who has not been helping matters tried all he could to make sure that he discourages every effort towards having warlords and people who could resurrect the buried course of avenging for the entire kingdom in general and its fallen heroes who were termed, deviants. There and then, the unfortunate lepers through the strict connivance of the traditional ruler gradually and eventually conquered the entire kingdom and became their lords spiritual and temporal. They dictated the tune in which every political, social, and economic activity of the entire kingdom must be conducted. Just as it is said that "he who pays the piper, dictates the tune", things started taking another shape from what they used to be.

The trend of events started taking different shapes. The pendulum was swinging in favor of the whites. But a few spirited individuals still could not hide their feeling about the turning of things. Some even vowed that no duty, no relation, and no religion, shall in any way separate them from their known and reverend cultures, irrespective of the pressures mounted on them. In fact, some elderly people and almost all the younger generation of the kingdom were not comfortable with the turning of things or the trend of events in a kingdom that has known peace and enjoyed communalism for a very long time before the advent of the whites. The people complained bitterly that, they were forcefully divorced from their good cultural ethos to marry a strange culture that they may not learn how to practice even to the end of their lives without coming to terms with its practice. Therefore, they vowed never to get married to this strange culture even though the knife of the traitor is closely held to their throats.

However, through the traditional ruler, law and order was to a greater extent, maintained to create a conducive atmosphere for the unfortunate lepers to carry out their exploitative businesses amicably. Although the more the traditional ruler tried to make the people blind or ignorant of the whole scenario, the more the people complained of the overheated exploitation to a near extinction of the whole kingdom. Yes of truth, it is said that "the best way to oppress people is to maintain the ignorance of the oppressed". But the case of this kingdom was a different ball game altogether.

And so, just as it is rightly said, "Any kingdom that is divided against itself shall fall". Also, it is said that "any society that stops to be a thinking society shall be a slave society". My son, this was how we became a slave in our father's land. So, this has been the story of our dear kingdom where we stay at the house of a feeble-minded person to point at the wasted compound of a fallen hero who through his efforts brought honor and prestige to our kingdom. Our dear kingdom is more or less a coward now because nothing motivates those heroic tendencies in us to achieve honor and glory in our kingdom.

My son as if that was not enough of man's inhumanity to man, the most unfortunate and disheartening thing to note about this trend of the event was that the unfortunate lepers tactfully and systematically transformed and stratified the kingdom into classes of people. Those who were supporting the tyranny and authoritarian leadership of the unfortunate lepers through the traditional ruler as a result of frustration and helplessness under the guise of "if you can't beat them" were graciously and religiously supplied with every life's good things. Their children were sent overseas for western education and they were now the haves of the kingdom in all strata. People who were not known in any of the villages in the kingdom. "They never do wells" of the kingdom, who were unable to take good care of their families were tactfully and systematically transformed to be leaders of the people. Well, it was not surprising because it was claimed by a man that, he saw slaves on horses and princes walking on foot. O! Where on earth do people imagine that one can give out what one doesn't have?

In fact, to further frustrate the people the more and heighten and perpetuate this "man's inhumanity to man" and also to further widen the gap between the considered "haves" and "have not", those who were sheepishly in support of the unfortunate lepers out of frustration and helplessness were carved out of the kingdom and they constituted the new settlement called, Uhu Ohum, closer to the camp of the unfortunate lepers, where they were comfortably living in luxury. To be very frank, so many feeble and fickle-minded people were sheepishly deceived and converted to the new fold readily, because they know they had nothing to offer to the meaningful development of the kingdom. Good a thing, many more people stuck tenaciously to their old ways of life which they consider far better and more enjoyable than the newly introduced way of life because its foundation was based on the concept of deceit and exploitation.

To this effect, the unfortunate lepers made sure that nothing good goes in and did not expect anything good to come out of our kingdom considered to be defiled because we refused to adopt the new faith. But one thing that puts the unfortunate lepers into confusion is that the people of the considered defiled kingdom were not side-attracted by whatever thing that was going on in the other camp. They were highly focused. They carried their cross gallantly and were not attracted by whatever was seen on the other camp of the kingdom. Happily, the people as united put up a bold front in defending their dignity as a people and were also undaunted and fully determined to be a free people. They strongly refused to believe that they were doomed to be the serfs and peons of the unfortunate lepers and the people of the other camp of the kingdom. The more the unfortunate lepers try to intimidate and exploit the people, the more the people are untied and committed to their course.

These unfortunate lepers were very surprised at this wonderful development and wondered about our people's source of courage, inspiration, and power. To this effect, they launched their first ideology, the two Cs: meaning, "if you can't convince them, confuse them" in the name of "brainwashing" education. In this circumstance, oh it was too appalling that those who were unstintingly patriotic, resolute, brave, and religiously committed to the course of their freedom were termed hoodlums; the actual hoodlums were termed saints, and the looters and betrayers in the name of leaders were termed God's sent. Therefore, based on this false and stage-managed premise, the entire operating system was nothing to write home about. This scenario made lepers to be reapers and corpers, the villagers, and paupers.

CHAPTER 5

Some ignorance is demonic.

Structurally speaking, and as if this was not enough evil and "man's inhumanity to man", the unfortunate lepers strategized on how to perpetually keep our people under their dominance through forced labor and a "divide and rule" system as a working principle for their ideological orientation, the two "CS," Hence, in the course of building their residential buildings in their camp, they forcefully conscripted our men in all spheres of these endeavors. Through forced labor, their camp was established. Other networks were actualized like the railways and road networks. However, this was a strategy aimed at weakening the strength of our workforce and also weakening the strength of our people's unity.

The crux of the matter here was that this strategy denuded our kingdom of vital manpower and left a lopsided deposited demographic balance unable to cope with the harsh tropical elements in the development processes. The system, however, expropriated much of the irreplaceable stock of highly valuable natural resources (i.e. minerals and wealth) which are the important foundation for economic development. It appropriated to a small elite (consisting of mostly its members, race or power disposition) a disproportion of capital share of the economy especially future land.

It is imposed by both direct price incentives and by direct physical and fiscal cohesion, a structure of production and specialization dictated by demand patterns and strategic requirements which were external to our economics and beyond our influence. Production factors of land, labor, and social institutions were directed to satisfy external ones. It also created a set of the administrative institution which not only undermined local traditional democratic processes but were eminently unsuited for motivating and mobilization of the kingdom for the real task of massive mobilization of the communities for sustainable development. Finally, it destroyed an essentially humanist value system that inherently reconciles material development with moral virtue and social justice.

In this circumstance, the loss of this value system constituted the most disheartening and annoying part of this pathetic story. During this dreadful venture, so many people from our camp lost their dear lives. Frankly speaking, the unfortunate lepers were technologically and technically advanced and equipped. They had so much equipment to work with, including some sophisticated machines, which they were using to make edifices in their street and strategic parks and gardens throughout the whole kingdom at their camp.

After a day's work, the director of works through their supervisors who were from the new settlement and who also know some of the stronger and vibrant young men from the perceived defiled kingdom who could stir up the people against the present social and economic order were frequently earmarked for this evil venture. The supervisors shall thus direct some of these helpless and defenseless workers they have earmarked for some of the edifices and shall station them at those points and places they want them to be in the guise that is where they shall receive their pay for the work well done.

These unsuspecting helpless and defenseless workers will patiently be waiting for their respective payments, since, it is rightly said that "a labourer deserves his wages". But when all are well stationed, they will be asked to stay there and never to leave the point they are kept for that point is the point the payer shall come to pay them and that, anyone who leaves his position shall not be paid. And, as soon as the supervisors are gone, they will send signals to the unfortunate lepers and they shall then beam the sophisticated machine towards those who have been stationed in those strategic areas. This sophisticated machine has the power to turn any mortal man into a molded edifice when the light from the machine is shone around you. And so, when these helpless, tired, and hungry workers will be hopefully waiting patiently for their pay packages, all of a sudden, a light shall shine around them and immediately they shall turn into a molded edifice. O! what a hopelessly terrible situation. They were not paid for the work they have religiously performed and at the same time, they were forced to go to the great beyond, causing the kingdom to shortage of manpower. And so, the population of our people was also being reduced on daily basis.

Our kingdom all day long continued to complain about the mysterious missing of their people. Precisely, there was never a day that, the number of people who go to work returned the same. And it was always the strongest among them who would not come back. All these were done to us to further frustrated our efforts, reduce our population and weaken our strength. Our people attribute this to the handiwork of the unfortunate lepers but could not hold on to anything as proof of this.

Yes, they had nobody to complain to. Their traditional ruler no longer listens to the yearnings of the people he is ruling over. They had no other place to make consultations because the unfortunate lepers, as soon as they took over everything from our people and through the devil incarnate decrees of the traditional ruler, utterly destroyed all our tradition and customs which constituted our belief system. They did not only destroy all our holy temples and places but also ruthlessly hanged all the priests of these holy temples accusing them falsely and portraying them as agents of backwardness and a symbol of incivility in the kingdom.

They, through the traditional ruler, who is now well versed in the principle of the two, "Cs", if you can't convince them, confuse them, and his cohorts burnt down all our holy temples together with everything therein. Also, they destroyed all symbols of worship in the kingdom and termed them "marks of slavery and primitivism". To this effect, our people did not bat an eyelid and did not border about what the alien lepers do to them. Just like what the grasses did in the forest when they had no one to complain to about their painful situation, they had a council on their own. The grasses said that "it was not the rains from heaven that torture them most.

In fact, according to them, they do not feel the pain because they do not know the source and therefore consider the tortures as fair trials. But the one that pains them most, is the rains that fall from the big tree which almost always press their mouth to the ground". And so, they decided never to grow under big trees. Impliedly, the big trees were then exposed to the direct rail of sunlight which eventually caused havoc to the big trees and they started withering, indicating that there must be a savior and a solution to every condition or situation.

In this circumstance, these destructions had a side effect on all those villagers who worked with the unfortunate lepers. From the traditional ruler to the last man on the list. They individually lost their first and last born of each family that was involved and a few were spared for the last doom that shall befall them. But the unfortunate lepers were free from these plagues because they studied the entire kingdom very well and schooled the people also very well through the people who out of greed and selfishness betrayed and sold their fatherland to the impostors who were very apprehensive of the power of these gods. And just as it is said that "the river does not drown who never touched his feet on it" they were exempted from these plagues. Frankly speaking, they sorted and wanted more of a way to subjugate and subject our people to their perpetual kingship and as soon as this was achieved because of their working principle, yes, they were able to strive for the people stack naked of all powers.

They were completely in charge. They take absolute control of the entire kingdom in all spheres of life with relative ease. However, just as it was believed by the people that everything about the unfortunate lepers was false, they also established and instituted their mark of slavery on a false premise called the church. This was regarded as the second ideology which had its working principles. One may be tempted to ask, is this not a paradoxical assault on the sanctity of humanity, that, a man who was hell-bent on, and devoted to eradicating all forms of slavery and primitivism, rather to a greater extent, impliedly amplified and unified it into one bold umbrella called church. It was disheartening to note that so many people were deceived by this new way and many more who gratified their heart desire termed it justification for joining the new way as they hinged their shameless art of betrayal on the maxims of "if one can't beat them, one joins them". Now, they won our brothers, and our kingdom can no longer act as one.

These traitors put a knife on the things that held us together and we have fallen apart. The underlying assumption of their working principle was that, the so-called superior race, called, the "haves" shall continue to soar higher, but the so-called inferior race, christened the "have not" even the little they have shall be collected from them and be added to those who already have. The most disheartening thing about this relationship was that they told us that the first shall be the last and that, no bastard shall enter heaven which impliedly meant that no commoner so to speak shall find enjoyment in all his toils on earth. They insinuated that whatever our people do is for the pleasure of the unfortunate lepers. O! what a shame! To make sure they dealt with us very well, they established schools and snatched our younger generation from us. Our children never grew up with us. And just as it is generally believed, that, "these unfortunate lepers have rejected a group of people trained by madmen and they turn the world upside down", they trained our children in like manners.

They exploited us to the point that, even the little we had as reserves were collected from us as our children's fees for giving them western education. They teach these children laziness in school because when they come back from school, they are always engaged with one assignment or the other which will hinder them from helping their parents on the farm. And so, on Sunday all roads lead to the church where they do the highest exploitation. Secularly they tax us and everything we have in the name of income and property taxes. In the church, they tax our women and children in the name of tithes. And this trend of events separated us from our children and they never grew with us. And so, things continued this way for a very long time because of our ignorance, which one man summarizes to be devilish because it has made life a bane for the greatest number of our population; and this has gone a long way to support or buttress the saying that "some ignorance is demonic."

To this end, the young boy breathed a deep sigh of relief and calmly asked his father, how many times does a man die. The father said once. The boy smiled and said, "father I disagree with you, because from the evidence before me and from my experience if experience in anything to reliably go by, it does not seem to me that a man dies once. But when a man who fully understood his mission on earth dies, his spirit lives on opting to be allowed to either continue or complete his mission on earth. And this is my story and my song all the day long." He continued, "father, from this day on, I have assumed my position and resumed my work. And if truly I am a recantation of that Great warlord, let his spirit come upon me and let the two supernatural assist me to achieve this for the entire kingdom for I have presented myself a sincere and worthy vessel for the work."

CHAPTER 6

Any society that stops being a thinking society, shall be a slave society

Two days later, as Nwachi was alone meditating on his mission, he fell into a trance, and behold, he found himself at his grandmother's compound where people gathered and were enjoying and entertaining themselves with a keg of palm wine. At the end of the enjoyment, it was time to pour out wine in libation, and a woman was given the last cup of the wine for this. The boy immediately took offence because it was unheard of and it has never happened anywhere on earth for a mere woman to pour out wine in libation. Without delay, he took his leave because he did not want to be part of that type of history. As soon as he got to the playground, he saw one old man, very old with grey hair all over his body seated on a well-carved round chair called, Ekweke, bitterly checking his legs and waging his head in agony.

The boy quickly ran to him, knelt before him, and calmly asked, Father, why are you feeling so bad and forsaken? What is the matter with you? Please I promise to be of great help to you before you do yourself any harm because the way you are seated is enough to signal that you are ready for anything. The old man breathed a deep sigh of relief and said, my son, gone are the days when trees were the land of squirrels. To be very frank, it is now I know that things have fallen apart, and consequently the centre can no longer hold. It is now that we are seeing what these madmen of the west have done to us. Life is no longer worth living and we are happily beckoning on the spirit of death to come and take us home, because, things that were generally considered taboos and eyesores are now everyday happenings and nothing is being done about them. Rather, it is on the increase and the perpetrators of these evils are proud and they are praised. Already, to the best of our knowledge, the crux of the matter is that almost everything is lost to these unfortunate lepers.

But the most disheartening thing about this case is that one wouldn't imagine where on earth a mere woman will pour out wine in libation. The boy jumped up and exclaimed what an eyesore! Father this was what made me leave where we gathered because I can't imagine that a mere woman will have the gut and audacity to pour out wine in libation. I decided not to be part of this new generational history. But what is happening to us and what does this suppose to mean? How long shall they continue to kill our prophets and we stay by the side and look; can't we do something now to salvage our society? The old man said, well, young boy, I have seen honesty in you and for this singular reason, let me tell you the implication of what this means.

Our land has been gradually raped and systematically reduced to nothing or so relegated to the background that, even a woman is more militant and harmful than us because those who are representing us do not reason and are not representing us well. You see, "any society that refuses or stops to be a thinking society, shall always be a slave society". How could one imagine a man who is set to undertake any venture wouldn't ask his fathers to pour out wine in libation for him but will go to the oracle they called the church and kneel done at the altar before everyone, and mere woman and uncircumcised males, children, will place their hands on his head for prayers. Where on earth will the prayers of such feeble and fickle-minded people as these work? In this circumstance, the boy shouted, for this reason, I have presented myself as a worthy sacrifice and atonement for salvaging this unfortunate situation of my people. O!

No wonder our great warrior shouted O! My society, who shall save thee? On my honour as a son of the soil and not only a descendant but also a reincarnation of the great warrior, I promise to save my people from this mess by my fist and as the two supernatural shall be with me. There and then, he consoled the old man and assured him of the victory of good over evil, and begged to leave. It was heartily granted and left.

And as he was on his way out of the old man's presence, his eyes were opened and he shouted, I shall make it as long as the two supernatural shall be with me. I am not afraid of the powers of the unfortunate lepers. whatever the source of their powers might be, it cannot stop me from achieving this for my kingdom because they have dealt cruelly with us. This is the time for us to emancipate ourselves from this fettered freedom and regain the departed glory of our kingdom. Finally speaking, just as it is said "a crusader is a spokesman of the inarticulate, a friend of the forgotten men and women of the society, a champion of the oppressed and a maker of history"; therefore, a good crusader, the young man started preaching the good news of "real freedom", not "fettered freedom".

He taught people how they could change their "freedoom" situation to real freedom. He explained "freedoom" in this context to mean, "dogmatically but freely accepting a freaky doctrine under the guise of civilization or modernization, from someone one thinks superior to, or feels inferior of, under suspected uncommon human traits and sheepishly or foolishly rejecting one's cultural and moral ethics, in the lying pretense of being civilized which eventually brings doom to the faithful and the entire society or inflict retardation into the entire processes of development of both human and the society. Accordingly, this scenario paves the way for the self-acclaimed free "Dons" to take advantage of this failure to siphon the society's commonwealth to build up a formidable political structure that takes the intervention of the Almighty God to dismantle.

His theme was "teach a youth to have faith in his ability; to believe that he is equal to the people of other races of mankind, mentally and physically; to look at no man as his superior or feel inferior of any man; teach the youth also to know that he may succeed if nobody else believes in him, but that he will never succeed if he doesn't believe in himself". To this end, as his preaching was attracting the attention of almost everybody in the kingdom, he called for a solemn assembly. To this effect, he tactfully encouraged the elders to take heart and be prayerful for the two supernatural are all out to salvage their unfortunate and ugly situation prompted by a few people's greed and selfishness. He emphatically told them that every road must have an end. And that coming events must cast their shadow on the wall of history, and that is only fools that can fail to decipher the handwriting on the wall of destiny. He continued, "Actually we are in this mess because of some people, thus, we shall come out of it by the relentless efforts of some people. And at end of the meeting, so many people willingly opted to be part of this new development. But he happily selected seven able-bodied young men.

For a short while, he led a very powerful delegation to the traditional ruler's palace where they met with the traditional ruler and his council of chiefs. Frankly speaking, he was the mouthpiece of the noble delegation. To this end, he did not appeal to the traditional ruler and his council of chiefs. Rather, he authoritatively told them that their time is up and that they should lift their course on the people to resurrect that old-time religion that was good enough for the people of the kingdom. The traditional ruler on his part, though very surprised at this kind of boldness, told him that he should not try an impossibility by advising him not to behave like the sparrow who ate to the brim one day and challenged its chi, the creator, in a wrestling match. He equally told him about some people, mighty men of velour, who thought they could embark on this dreadful venture and succeed but eventually failed without achieving their respective goals because the powers that be were strongly and solidly against them.

He thought he could discourage them as usual by citing so many cases and finally but derogatorily said if these great men of valor failed woefully, then how can a riffraff and a pauper at his teens like you succeed? Then the boy boldly told him that they did not come to seek his opinion on the issue at stake but only wished that God will give him the tact to mend his ways so as not to stand on the ways of the two supernatural who in their infinite wisdom set the scenario in motion; for it is only a foolish dog that barks at a flying bird. This marked the end of the meeting and the delegation left the palace, leaving the traditional ruler and his council of chiefs behind. The council seriously marveled over that kind of boldness that radiated from the faces of the members of the delegation and deciphered the handwriting on the wall of history.

CHAPTER 7
Evil shall continue to exist,
whereas good people refuse to talk.

Frankly speaking, the boy did not sleep off this pertinent task from his mind. Accordingly, he mapped out strategies on how to tackle this task to achieve his noble objectives. He refused, among other things, to believe that they were doomed to be serfs and peons of others. He was resolute, determined, and focused. He believed that there was a need for a more positive action to liquidate these factors which make life a bane for the greatest number of his people. Therefore, he stepped into the case fully without minding the cost. He made secret plans on how to discover the secret behind the power of these unfortunate lepers. But unfortunately for this group, the new reformist group, the traditional ruler in conjunction with his cohorts on his part was also planning seriously on how to stop this group from achieving its objectives.

He termed them deviants and declared that their activities must be monitored and scrutinized. And at any point in time, it is found wanting that is, any action that is in any way against or challenges the leadership of the whites should be termed a treasonable felony and shall be punishable by death sentence. The traditional ruler also reported this new development to the authority of the whites, the powers that be. Immediately, the authority created new law courts and laws to guard against any youth revolt that may in any way disturb their exploitative businesses. And the only acceptable law to this effect was the rules which were made by the political superiors for the obedience of the political inferiors; because they understand, politics, as the art of governing others by deceiving them.

However, these new laws were not enough deterrence to the reformist movement. They believed that in some cases, faith is so often mocked in pop culture that gibbon could be seen as a radical, just for approaching the gospel with a straight face. Already it has been established that the people are deprived and marginalized. And, just as it is said" when a community is driven to the wall and in a situation of crisis where they have to fight for their right, they always fall back, in the past, on whatever resources they can use. As a structural response to the alarming and disheartening level of underdevelopment of the perceived defiled kingdom and the concomitant impoverishment of the masses of this region, the reformist group was undauntedly determined to foster order, stability, consensus, and habit to replace the prevailing condition of uncertainties, conflict of roles, challenges, and disorder that threaten to engulf the entire kingdom and under which no sustainable development has been and will ever be attained, without counting the cost.

Equally, they believed that there were two major things involved in the rabbit race, "if one does not succeed in killing the rabbit, one succeeds in destroying its hideouts". They were highly committed to this course in the belief that "to know is to understand, and to understand means to change, and to change equally means to develop". And so, they summarily supported this maxim which automatically became their watchword, "any man who has nothing that appeals to him to the extent of dying for such a thing should quit this planet earth and look for somewhere else to live".

With this conviction, they pledged to sacrifice their lives to salvage the ugly situation or bad condition of the entire kingdom. For this reason, the young boy promised the group that he was going to find out the secret behind the unfortunate lepers' powers. He fixed their next meeting in seven days to enable him to have enough consultation with the gods of the land. About midnight the following day, at the full of the moon, he came out of his room stark naked and went behind his father's reception hall where he knew nobody would hear what he shall be saying. He broke the kola nut he was having into pieces. He first called on God of heaven as the God of justice and source of all powers; he called on Ina Ajah, the great warrior known to them from generation to generation through whom and in whom other great warriors lived and died. He also called the seven warlords who founded the seven individual villages that made up the entire kingdom.

As he was calling on them, he was throwing out the pieced kola nuts until they got finished. In the end, he also called on their ancestors and all the spirit ruling the air, land, sea, and forest to come forth and fortify their hands, plans, and action to the effect of saving the entire kingdom from the cruel hands of the unfortunate lepers and the insults of their mad indigenous tyrants. And he exclaimed "O! That these people may know that no culture is superior or inferior to any other culture but that when two cultures meet, they should be allowed to strive on a free playing ground to effect modernity since it is believed that everything goes in pairs".

Then, he heard a voice that said, boy take heart for the course that you are fighting is the course of the two supernatural which was only pending because we were only searching for the right person who could do it perfectly well for us and now that the right person has emerged; and so everything is set for the project. However, we advise you to appear in this form tomorrow by twelve midnight at the playground for a communion with the two supernatural and it shall be well with the group. And he replied in humility, whatever my lord's spiritual and temporal wish I should do, I shall do it to the best of my ability. At this juncture, he went back to his room and slept. The following morning, he went about his normal business without disclosing his encounter with the gods to anyone.

By midnight according to the directive, he went to the playground with a kola nut and white chalk called, Nnzu, and as soon as he got there, his eyes were opened. He saw very old people seated around a very high stool, drinking palm wine. Fear almost gripped him because of the attire and mood these people were, but he comported himself and immediately he heard a call, inviting him to the big circle. He boldly entered the circle and was directed to where he should seat and it was at the foot of the high stool.

There and then, he made himself comfortably seated. And as if it were a dream, one of those old people seated in the circle served him wine as a way of welcoming him to the fold. When this was over, the higher deity who sat on the stool then said, young boy, you have been gotten today as a son and has been commissioned as the living representative of the two supernatural to go and set the captive free, even the captive of the might. Those who are living in bondage are now slaves in their father's land and shall be free by your efforts and sacrifices. So, no weapon known to man or ever fashioned by man, shall by any way hurt you throughout your lifetime. It shall not be for you or your boys. And whoever stands against you on this noble course shall surely die. Today, your commissioning has been sealed with this staff of office, and the staff was handed over to him by one of those people seated in the circle and that marked his official commissioning to this course, and the meeting ended, and he went back to his room with the staff of office.

At the dawn of the morning, the boy called his men to a very brief meeting where he told them that he was going into the camp of the unfortunate lepers to spy out the whole camp before they could strike. Although his men told him that it was a deadly mission but they had confidence in his abilities. Immediately, they pledged to join in the mission since they have pledged to live together and die together. But he told them that they should leave the task to him because the spying out of the camp must be directed by two supernatural. Without further delay, they all accepted to leave the task for the boy. Two days later, as he was going to the unfortunate leper's camp; at their junction, one madman was sitting. In this circumstance, a lawyer was coming from the other angle, and men from the governor's office were on the other side. At this juncture, everybody was claiming the right of way, they blocked the junction, and traffic jams started building up. People thought that the thing will soon be over because they were acclaimed as reputable men in society.

But contrary to their view, the situation persisted because none was willing to give way for others to pass. The madam rushed in between them, ordered the one on his right-hand side to go back and he obeyed, he ordered the one on his left-hand side to pull away to traffic, and the way was opened and people marveled at this brilliant act of the madman. Based on this scenario, the boy disguised himself as a complete madman unknown to anyone and made his way to the camp of the unfortunate lepers. Just like a real madman, he formed a song, and as he moved, the rhythm of the song will rhyme with his steps. And he sang, my brothers please help me and God shall bless you, I am a madman, I live in bondage, please my people pity me and save me from dying in my new state for it was not my fault but my brother's fault who sold me to state because of greed and inordinate ambition.

Frankly speaking, people were touched and willing to help him because of the song. But some people, at the sight of him, will continue to shrug and shout " the blood of Jesus" until he passes by because he looked very dreadful; and behind them, when they must have gone far away from him, he will say yes, I know you, at the seat of your enjoyment, you will not call Jesus but when you are in troubles and want to get one or two things that are bordering you done, you call Jesus. Well, God shall judge us individually according to our cultural ethics and work to humanity."

CHAPTER 8
Fools shall live to regret the
Words they speak but good
People/wise people shall live to
Regret the silence they keep.

And so, he continued throughout the whole camp. He was able to discover all the secret places of the camp and he plotted a good graph and map of the whole place indicating all the secret places and where their armour house is. He also discovered and marked the location of the sophisticated machine that has the capability of turning mortals into an edifice. In the end, he went out of the camp and presented his findings to his men, and they jointly drew up their next line of action. The first thing they did was to go again to the traditional ruler and told him that the time has come for him to lift his selfish course on the entire kingdom for it to know peace as it did in the beginning. But the traditional ruler laughed at them and said "I happily spite on your good for nothing effort because I have confidence in the extraordinary powers of the powers that be and to the best of my knowledge, no other power, in heaven or on earth or even beneath the earth, shall snatch their prey from their grip.

And so, there is no point trying impossibility. I know that young men are hell-bent on making history that could boost their ego. But I want you to know that you are not ripe enough to fight for this course. I am convinced and highly persuaded that you people, driven by youthful exuberance, just want to make names for yourselves as historic warriors of the kingdom, perhaps to be admired by some of our beautiful girls. I am emphatically saying that you should know that warriors are not known in the kingdom but kings are.

And I am assuring you that, so long as I am the honoueable king of this great kingdom, there is no way you can succeed in this plot. And as he wanted to continue this insult to this group and based on his boast, the young boy shouted, ''enough of this noise making of yours!'' And the king kept quiet. I am sorry he continued that you have gone out of your senses and your conscience is also dead because of the little fleeting pleasure of sin you think you enjoy from the crumbs that fell out from the table of the powers that be. Why must a man under-rate the supreme powers that shield him and the people who made him king over.

Well, the supreme powers are manifest in us and we are guided and directed by the yearnings of the people. Based on this, we shall in no distant time prove to the world that for any community or society on earth to reach the acme of greatness and respectability, it is not quantity that counts but quality and the type of people who make up the society. The fair play, justice, and the white man's word of honour which were falsely quoted as the working principle of their second ideological orientation which you and your cohorts loved so dearly and cherished as long as you live are meaningless to us in general and to me in particular because it is all deceit.

However, we just want to tell you that we love our fatherland very dearly and by the help and grace of the two supernaturals, it is solidarity forever. We shall remain and continue to grow, live, and always act like truly brave and one people for all time. Remember "those whose palm kernels were cracked by some benevolent spirits should not only learn how to be humble but also be gracious and gratefully responsible, frugal, prudent, accountable and accommodating". Although, they say that ''the way a man attains power, dictates the way he relates with or attends to his superiors, equals, and subordinates. But remember, freedom brings peace, and liberation brings development.

And, because you have decided to stubbornly stand on the ways of the two supernatural, you shall lose everything you think you have religiously acquired. Your life and that of your entire family shall be worthy sacrifices for actualizing our freedom because it is always that, the sheep that bleat too much makes itself prey and is always the target of the predators; when it bleats it will review its hidings and thus attracts predator and must be the first to be cut off from the fold. You may not understand what I am telling you now because you are still in your old self but sooner or late, you will understand the better by and by.''

These words stretched the patience of the traditional ruler and out of fierce anger, he ordered the reformist team to leave his presence but before they left, the young boy said, "Yes the human conscience has always had the potent capacity to reverse the act of man's inhumanity to man, the evil done by man to man will be redressed, if not now then certainly later…. that the triumph of evil over good can only be temporary because lies have short legs. We don't blame you but we blame your ignorance because human being is ignorant. That is why in many parts of the world they regard power as an end, instead of a means of bringing happiness to many.

Human beings are greedy. That is why those who have the good things of life are not only bent on having more but they go to the extent of depriving those who have not, even, that little which they have, are forcefully taken from them to be added to the greedy haves.

Yes, we do not blame you too much but we blame your greed and selfish nature because it is said that "man is a product of nature and nurture. And it is based on this, that it could be correct to say, that society corrupts man if his conscience is dead. However, man was a good thing to the creature but it is said that "if a goat messes up where it stays, then standing up becomes the next and better option for it". You have messed up where you stay, then " a bird can't be steady when it perches on an unsteady tree". Therefore, be warned, everything has a price!" Have a nice day and the team left the presence of the traditional ruler.

Immediately, the traditional ruler also without delay left his palace and made his way to the camp of the whites to report this surprising challenge and the kind of embracement he received from a little team of seven. But unfortunately for him, as he was just resting his case, the leader and mouthpiece of the team dressed in the native war attire appeared and made serious advances toward them. The traditional ruler shouted, the troubler of the entire kingdom what have you come here to seek? The young boy said, I am not the troubler but you and your cohorts are. Well, that is not the issue for now, but I have come to let the unfortunate lepers know that their time is up for them to give back the land and all that is in it to its rightful owners in peace or conquest. We graciously give them 24 hours, to do this or face the unpleasant consequences at the end of the 24 hours, for we provide a great store of commitments to this noble course.

To be very frank, this was a very dangerous and deadly signal to the dynasty of the whites and was not taken for granted. As soon as the young boy left unharmed they plotted how to get this team of seven destroyed. The traditional ruler begged that they should mobilize him with the state fiat to enable him to use his good offices as the traditional ruler to track them down. That was done immediately and the whole thing started in earnest. The traditional ruler called all stakeholders to a very brief meeting and in the end; they allegedly accused this team of treason and cultivating the "culture of opposition" to the powers that be. And they concluded that such must be squarely dealt with, just as they did to the priest of their holy temples and places. An emergency call was made, the whole kingdom gathered, and the case of this team was presented. This raised so many problems and the entire kingdom was divided into two camps.

The camp led by the traditional ruler and his cohorts did not only suggest imprisonment but also passed a death sentence on the team. While the other side consisting of the poor and defenseless masses together with others or those who were now considering themselves as slaves in heaven were of the candid opinion that the team should be left untouched. There was a very big problem that almost resulted in communal war between the proper villagers and the would-be villagers if not for their ancestral ties. However, the only thing that saved the situation was that the traditional ruler quickly discovered that they would lose the war because his domain was divided against itself on the issue at stake. To this effect, one of the eldest men from the perceived "pauper kingdom" according to the "deceived kingdom" sued for an audience and there was a dead silence. He continued my people o! how long shall we continue to be deceived and fooled by these unfortunate lepers? Frankly speaking, the fault is all ours because, when they came, they got us by us, schooled us through us, rearrange us to the best of their ability, and changed us to the best of their knowledge.

Based on this scenario, they exploited us to near extinction and left us almost desolate. Now their strategy is to gradually change our focus from them to pulling down ourselves while they stay by the side and look and claim they were helping us. But how long shall we continue this way? It is said that "a fool at forty is a fool forever". We are mature enough to know that this man's inhumanity to man in the guise of governance is going against our throats. Therefore, if the two supernatural have remembered us and sent a messiah to us, we should be very happy to welcome them and not stand in their ways. In my humble opinion, I suggest that we should allow this team to be if it were from man, it will not succeed and we shall all see it, but if it were from the two supernatural then who are we, mortal men to stop them? Please, my people, let us not strive against the wind, rather let us allow the sleeping dog to lie; let us be patient with time, and the team and the truth about their mission shall unfold in no distant time.

In this circumstance, it was carried by almost everybody in the gathering but the traditional ruler looked at it as resigning to fate and being defeated because of his boast. Having confidence in the power of the state fait at his disposal, he told the people openly that this controversial issue should be decided through voting to bring about democratic fair play and justice to bear in the case at hand. To this effect, the people of the other side of the camp faulted it and said "the majority carries the vote" syndrome of democracy is premised on falsehood because it is a calculated attempt to maintain the ignorance of the oppressed and to manipulate and maneuver things to the success or for the selfish gains of the political superiors. And so, they vehemently stood against it and promised that even though they see the knife of the traitors held closely to their throat that they cannot give up their opinion about the issue at stake, moreover as they counted this, the third deceit through which the unfortunate lepers maintain their dominance over the people of the kingdom.

In the end, the young boy and the leader of the team sued for an audience and there was a dead silence. He continued, yes, we make compromises just to allow the society to succeed; without compromise, could this wide world of ours progress? When two incompatibles meet, they co-exist by agreeing to agree on certain issues and agreeing to disagree on other issues. I just want the traditional ruler and his cohorts to know that compromise is the art of symbolic living; hence the most successful leaders are those who compromise for the common good while not sacrificing fundamental principles. But let him and his cohorts know that the existence of the state depends on the goodwill of the people for the state, just as the existence of the people depends on the goodwill of the state for the people. The relationship is like an equation of two sides, and the two sides must be balanced before it could be called a complete equation. Although the conscience of the traditional ruler and his cohorts are dead, not only poisoned by the inducement from the unfortunate lepers; but since it is possible that the bones could rise again, I heartily prophesize to their souls and conscience to rise again and be attuned to the yearnings of the masses, and also to acknowledge the fact that we are expected to bind the society's wound and heal it with breaches of the past, so that in forging our great kingdom ahead, we shall emerge on the slate of history hate-free and agreed-free people."

However, he continued, for its practicality, while human beings can rationalize any topic, move, wisdom, and commonsense dictates that life can be more meaningful by compromising idealism to approximate what is the truth. Therefore, it is said that "part of wisdom lies on changing those things that can be changed and accepting those things that can't be changed". Nevertheless, in my honor as the leader of this team and the initiator of this program, I have heard enough words concerning this movement but I want to say that I have heard the new order. The battle line is drawn, then we can all go back home and die in humiliation, to strictly comply with the new order from the powers that be. But for me, I shall go to any length to restore the kingdom's prestige and dignity at the sacrifices of my life for the second time. And if I may ask, who shall go back home and who shall go with me? And the entire kingdom shouted in unison, we shall all go-o-o to retrieve back our inheritance and the whole place became very rowdy and the traditional ruler and his cohorts saw the handwriting on the wall early enough and disappeared, thus, the meeting ended as traditional ruler and his cohorts quickly rushed home.

CHAPTER 9
"Freedom is complete when it
Address the issues of fear asFreedom of
conscience; wants Freedom of economy;
and Protection as political freedom."

To this effect, the traditional ruler quickly but fearfully ran to the white man's camp to report the latest development so far. He painstakingly narrated all that happened at the meeting to them and also emphatically told them that, the battle line is drawn and that they should intervene as quickly as possible to stop this sad trend event. Without delay, the powers that be decided to use the state mercenaries to track them down. At first, the team was arrested by a team police army, but the villagers for the first time intervened but that was more fire, more blood, and much death. Even at that, the villagers were willing to die than see this team taken away by this joint team of armed men. In this circumstance, having seen the number of people who were dead already, the number of people wounded, and the willingness of the people to die more, the boy told the people that he shall go to exile to distract the attention of the state and the powers that be. He asked his men to go back to their respective homes and be prayerful that in no distant time, the team shall come together to strike.

And so, the entire kingdom and the team of armed men who came to arrest them witnessed the excursion far into the forest and they parted. The joint team of the armed men went back to the people who sent them and reported the latest development. And that called for merriment having dislodged the perceived trouble-makers of the kingdom. So, they wined and dined happily throughout the day in what they called a cocktail party. The villagers on their part mournfully poured out wine in libation that the two supernatural shall guide and protect their seen savior till the time sets for the last battle. Then the team regrouped and were seriously preparing for the last battle. The powers that be heartlessly increased the suffering and labor of the people by trying to use hunger as an instrument of war to wipe out the whole kingdom by blocking all borders through which food gets to the village and consequently increased their labor and taxation. But the villagers did not bat an eyelid. Happily, they made do with the little they had because they believed that their salvation was nearer to them than before; coupled with the fact that "any hungry man who has hope of eating in no distant time shall not die". And so, life continued. However, the boy in exile was getting refreshed day in and day out and also stronger for the battle ahead. Therefore, having known what the war will look like, he made provisions for where all the villages shall relax and wait for their victory over their enemies.

However, as the whole people were feeling for him, one fateful day as he was coming back from his daily business, one of his disciples, chinecherem who was sent by his people and also instructed in the dream by the gods of the land to go for him, fortunately, met him at omogwu, where two streams meet, very close to the brook of okpasue, where he was in forceful exile. He was very happy to see him because it was an indication that the time has come but actually, he did not show this in his countenance. He received him, that is, they exchanged pleasantries and he took him down into the Brook where he lived. He presented one bottle of illicit gin with a wine cup made of calabash called, Ntico, to his august visitor.

Chinecherem quickly without being told took the lead in sharing the wine. He, first of all, poured the first cup of wine and gave it to him. He stood up well from his well-carved Ekweke chair, his spirit was vexed to a point that tears for the first time in the history of his life rolled down his cheeks. His disciples shouted and went down on his kneels before him, holding his heels, my lord, he said, what must have caused tears to drop from your eyes even at this point that the battle was over? But he exclaimed, God of heaven, the gods of our land, I am sure you are not dead; our ancestors, the fathers of this kingdom, I am sure you are still living as heroes in the land of the dead because you were heroes of your time on earth; but when shall we salvage, rebuild and restore the lost glory of this great kingdom.

"How do you expect us to patiently watch these imposters and wretched lepers destroy our culture and all that made us people of distinct features in history through the hands of our unfaithful and greed-ravaged brothers who out of sheer selfishness and crass stupidity sold their birthright and fatherland to aliens who in turn made us complete slaves and tenants in our fatherland! O! How can a man be relegated so low to the background, even to the point of being a complete woman that he cannot feel the pause of those who scream and yearn for salvation? Therefore, I stand on my feet and in tears for the first and last time to call on the two supernatural to come to our aid for now is the time. He looked up to the heavens, swallowed hard, and tearfully poured out the wine in libation and handed over the cup to his visitor. He collected the cup quickly and refilled it with wine again and directed it to him, but he asked him to take the first part of the wine as tradition demanded. He obeyed immediately. He took the wine and then put another one for him. He then took his share and also ordered his visitor to refill the cup again, and he complied without delay.

The boy then cleared his throat and tactfully said, yes, my friend, brother, and partner in the noble race, what brought you to my hideout? He did not want to waste any more time, he quickly opened up and was straight to the point. He told him without mincing words that his people and the gods of their land want him back immediately for the iron is now hot to be stricken. And as he was at pains to fully narrate how his people dearly want him back and his encounter with the gods and their ancestors in the dream that prompted his visit, the boy sprang up as if he was controlled through a remote, he went into the inner part of the brook and packed all his belongings together and brought them out before him. This action cut his words short and he was carefully watching him.

Then when he eventually sat down, he said, please, my brother and friend this should be enough indication that I have heard all that you have just said. Truly speaking, I just want to assure you that the time has come, and now is the time for us to invade the camp of the oppressors and possess our possessions. I am sorry, that I may not follow you immediately. But take my words to my people, tell them that presently my spirit is with them already. They shall see me in person as soon as I am through with my consultations. His disciple was very happy about a mission well fulfilled. He stood up from where he was sitting, knelt before him, and said, as my lord has commanded, I shall, to the best of my ability, carry it out perfectly well. However, I thank you so much for accepting this offer, and may the two supernatural continually be your guide till we meet. And he said, yes, my friend, that is the spirit. Well, let us keep our fingers crossed and our eyes wide open. Please one more cup for you and me before we call it a day. Yes, my lord, he complied promptly, and at the end of this, he saw him off and they happily parted in peace.

He come back to this brook and sat down quietly on his carved chair. A few minutes later, a cross-section of the two supernatural met with him and ministered to him. Chinecherem reached home happily and immediately all the elderly men who sent him on the errand, heard of his arrival and all gathered at one of the eldest man's houses, hoary Idikaeze. As soon as all who were expected to be present gathered, another elderly man in the gathering, hoary Udogadi opened up the solemn assembly with libation and opening prayer. Then, ichie Ongunu as chosen, cleared his throat and in the same vein invited their errand boy to come out and give them a comprehensive account of his mission to their illustrious son's hideout. He, Chinecherem, as a tested and trusted errand boy and an obedient disciple of their illustrious son, dramatically presented his mission. And as he was at pains narrating the success of his journey, the boy entered and greeted the people in their traditional way of joining a public gathering and they all responded happily. At that moment, the interruption cut Chinecherem's speeches short and there was a dead silence.

After some moment of silence as if they were giving a minute silence for his arrival, hoary Anyasor, cleared his throat gently and cheerfully greeted the people and they responded. Then, he continued, yes, my people, this has gone a long way to prove that our gods are not dead and our ancestors are not sleeping too. This also, to a very large extent, has proved to be true the successful story our beloved son Chinecherem was telling us. It has corroborated the successful story told us. Yes, it is said that, "when a diviner divines and explains his divination then that next?" The long-awaited messiah is here with us, so what do we tell him? As soon as he rested his case, hoary Udogadi followed suit. He, first of all, greeted the people and they responded. He continued, my people, it is said that "when all is ready for a project to be executed, waiting longer than necessary is dangerous". Our son, brother, and messiah, our eyes are on you, what is our next line of action?" Please we have given a license to address us.

The boy happily rose to the occasion, he, first of all, thanked them for having something more than faith in the course they were fighting together. And to this effect, he told them that victory is assured. He told them that everything was set for the battle and that they were not going to give their enemy any breathing space; that everything starts immediately. He ordered that all men be mobilized at the playground for the last briefing. This order ended their meeting. In a couple of hours, the playground was filled with people patiently waiting to be briefed. He came out without delay and addressed the gathering. He, first of all, thanks the whole people for their patience and for developing a very large heart to present a bold front on their common course. He continued, be of good cheer my brothers and compatriots. The struggle for our freedom may have been long and gloomy. But behind the cloud of suffering and disappointment loom the rays of hope and success on the distant horizon. So long as we refuse to believe that we are doomed to be the serfs and peons of others, our kingdom shall be redeemed, and we shall have a new life and enjoy it abundantly.

However, based on the fact that we have been able to discover and understand the unfortunate lepers' weakness and strength and vice versa, I want the entire kingdom to relocate to the brook of okpasue, where I have prepared for them, just to pass a night, and at the dawn of the morning, victory will be ours. This is because they know that we are invincible and so their target is the defenseless masses and this always weakens our strength and morale for this venture. Therefore, if the people of the kingdom shall comply strictly with us, by the grace of the two supernatural, the people shall not last more than a night in the brook. Finally, he declared that two of his men, Chinecherem inclusive, shall take the people of the kingdom to the brook. He pleaded that all families shall prepare well with enough food that may take them for a day for they shall take their lunch in their respective homes, the following day.

He conclusively said that those who supported them from the other camp of the kingdom shall also be taken along because they may be their next target. Immediately, three of his men were sent on this errand, and in no distant time, they came back and reported that the message has been delivered to the people it was meant for. And as proof of this, before they could finish reporting to the people who sent them, all who received the message started coming into the gathering. And after one or two comments from those who joined later, the meeting ended with a libation and closing prayer, pleading for journey mercies to the brook and victory over their enemies. And the meeting ended and the people parted and returned to their respective homes quietly.

CHAPTER 10

The better use of life is to spend it on something that outlasts life; because what we do for ourselves dies with us, but what we do to others and the world remains and it is immortal.

To this effect, preparations were going on in all quarters of the kingdom, and at about six o'clock in the evening of that day, every family was set for the exodus of the people to the brook of okpasue. Before half past six o'clock that same evening, those people and families from the other kingdom all arrived and the exodus started in earnest without delay. Actually, none lit the light until they were far into the forest which led to the book to avoid attracting the attention of the traitors to the new settlement. In a couple of hours, they happily got to the brook and discovered that the brook has the capacity of accommodating the entire kingdom put together and they settled there, family by family. The two men who led them down to the brook immediately took their leave to join their group. As soon as they saw these people, this was enough indication to show that the people of the kingdom have eventually relocated.

Happily, the team went to the playground and straight to the heart of the playground called omaogo known to the people as the assembly ground of their gods and ancestors. Without delay, they stood round the big tree there with each holding the other in form of a chain. As soon as this was done, the boy said in a still small voice, we are happy that you have found favour in us and have decided to make us worthy vessels for this course.

Yes, we are united in purpose, and putting up this bold front as thou has enabled us, we are striking this night in thy name. Fortify our hands into an iron fist and let us achieve our central objective, total emancipation, and freedom, before the dawn of the morning, to persuasively convince the entire kingdom that the battle was thou. Thanks for hearing us and we are out at your honorable command.

As soon as he was done with his speech, a gentle breeze blew across them and they were all fortified they picked up molded white chalk called, Nzu, from the foot of the big tree, individually as their shield and bulletproof before they embarked on the noble mission. At this juncture, it occurred to the boy to run down to the burnt iron god's temple to pick one of the keys there for the battle. He did that immediately and joined the team. From there, they moved. They ran as if they were horses and in a couple of hours, they were at the gate of the unfortunate lepers' camp. Good a thing, the gate was not yet locked. They entered and used their padlock to lock the gate. But unfortunately for the team, they did not know that all members of the camp have not come in, particularly the patrol guards of the camp.

Frankly speaking, the unfortunate lepers were down to earth taken unawares, and never expected that the war will take the form it took. However, when they saw these armed men moving like horses in speed, they signaled the patrol guards outside the camp who came immediately according to their training to the gate and discovered that it was locked from the inside. Meanwhile, these horse-like –men had already taken over the control of their armory and that sophisticated machine that has the capacity of turning every mortal being into a monumental edifice. Having the map of the whole kingdom intact, within ten minutes, they were able to overpower and dislodge all who were guards to these strongholds and have all of them in chains. In these circumstances, the patrol guards outside were directed to invade the villages or camps of their perceived enemies and shoot at sight any living being there, both men and animals. But unfortunately for them, they got there and did not see even a domestic animal to shoot. They quickly rushed to the new settlement they knew in search of these people but it was an exercise in futility.

Precisely speaking, what they saw greatly surprised them. They discovered to their utter dismay that even the new settlement was empty. They did not give it a second thought and thereby concluded that it was the plot of the traditional ruler and his cohorts. And so, without any atom of mercy, they summarily rounded off the entire family members of the traditional ruler and his dear cohorts without listening to any appeal or plead for mercy and without sparing even one member to continue their lineages and also set their houses and property ablaze and there was a great inferno. And as there was a shout of cry and shooting in the other camp, the team which did not intend to kill anyone then decided to call these heartless and crazy murders to order by ruthlessly slaughtering some of the guards they held captive and also in retaliation to what was exactly going on in the other camp. Immediately an order was issued to the guards to surrender and retreat, and that was done without delay.

To this end, the leader of the team declared that all mature men in the kingdom should come out to one of the largest open fields they called, parks and gardens, for man-to-man open confrontation. They all came out in a tremble, but as they came forth, they sued for peace, they held French leaves. Eventually, the leader of the team gave them options for long-lasting peace in the kingdom. Without delay, they accepted it with all pleasure, out of fear, and the first part of these conditions or options was immediately carried out. All their strongholds were summarily burnt down and at this juncture, the leader immediately rushed to the gate, opened it and ushered those patrol team outside in by himself and matched them down with their weapons on them to one of the burning points, and threw all the weapons they had into the inferno.

However, when the first condition or option was going on, he called out the second option which was burning down all their churches, courts, and prisons which was a retaliation to what they did to their holy temples and places. This was also to serve as a way of destroying perpetually the western mark of slavery and dominance over the people of the kingdom in all ramifications. Finally, also a way of reuniting and reintegrating the entire kingdom into a hate-free and greed-free society from the disorganized and rivalry-ravaged territories. Yes, without delay, they set all the churches, courts, and prison yards ablaze because they have been disarmed and forced to sincerely sue for peace. However, before this was completed, it was about five O'clock in the morning and the leader of the team happily sent one of his men to go and tell their people that the battle was over.

Immediately, he complied strictly with this order. When he got there, most of the people were still sleeping but some were already awake. He quickly cornered some of those mature men who were awake and told them about their victory. They, to some extent, doubted the good news or report, but happily sent two able-bodied young men to go and see to themselves, because it is said that "the witness of one man cannot establish a fact to be true, but by the witnesses of two or more people, a case or fact is established as true".

Without delay, they complied and as they got there, they saw to themselves that it was indeed true. They happily returned to their camp with a song of victory. Good a thing, before they could happily get to their camp, the people and place were already agog and delighted with the good news. They went in happily and corroborated the story and there was a shout of joy in the camp.

Because of this, the people were all happily set to return to their fatherland as owners and landlords and no longer as slaves highly exploited by the exploiters. However, before the people started arriving in the kingdom, the team of seven was already at the playground waiting to happily welcome them. Precisely speaking, before eight O' clock that fateful morning, the people of the kingdom from partial exile had all arrived in the kingdom and were received by the team with a heart-renting sound of the great Ikoro drum. To this effect, the leader and mouthpiece of the team presented their welcome address which summarily read thus:

"we are grateful to God of heaven and the gods of our dear land for their joint efforts towards actualizing this dream. We thank the two supernatural for the grace and enablement given to us throughout our quest and struggle for freedom from the fettered freedom. We are particularly happy for the collective and individual sacrifices made in lieu of this. Let us all remember what it took the entire kingdom to achieve her freedom.

Therefore love the brotherhood so dearly to enable us to maintain this pace and the pace we shall so set for ourselves as to enhance and also facilitate our making meaningful progress now and in time to come. And for us to be happier, let us from this point build an integrated kingdom with a centralized administration and efficient personalities from the disorganized and rivalry-ravaged territory as the two supernatural have opened up a new page for us. And so, at this first and fresh start, let us pursue the policy of cautious neutrality to escape the pressure of rival powers that may want to emerge. God bless our new kingdom. He concluded his speech and greeted the people and they answered with meticulous zeal, and there were a lot of cheers there.

At this juncture, Ichie Echendu happily greeted the people craving their indulgence, good a thing they answered and there was a dead silence. He continued rather in an exaggerated way, saying, actually our gods have come down to us in the name or form of this team of seven, for apart from them who else would have achieved this laudable victory for us in a twinkle of an eye?

Frankly speaking, in the history of humanity, I have not seen anywhere on earth that the success and salvation of a race were achieved by so few people with less stress and less blood. Precisely speaking, I am not trying to pour so much encounim on them, but I am particularly happy that this has gone a long way, to prove that their quest and earnest desire for freedom was not of men but God as quoted by one of our noblest sons.

Well, if an old man mournfully seats with a keg of palm wine appealing to the gods of their land and ancestors on behalf of his son who went out for war. And all of a sudden, he sees the son coming back home happily with some human heads on him, what do you think is expected of the old man? And there was a shout of joy, honor, and celebration among them.

He paused for a while, frowned with total concentration, and greeted the people, they happily answered with a meticulous zeal and there was a dead silence. He continued, my people, I am particularly happy because every living soul here even the dead ones of the kingdom is aware of the terrible tribulation, in fact, the hell and hard water we passed through which has now indicated that in the darkness there must surely come out light. Yes, they told us that life was all about the survival of the fittest and that it was only the fit of the fittest that shall survive; thereby instigating fear in us and seducing us with flattery not to take action.

Thank God one can only stop people from taking action but one cannot stop people from reasoning. I am happy that I am alive today to see with my two naked eyes the salvation of the kingdom which turned us from a slave society to a thinking society. Therefore, even if I join my good ancestors after this speech, I shall go home happy because I think I have good news for them.

Well, I rest my case here to enable other nobles to speak on this great achievement he greeted the people and they answered and there were cheers.

Another elderly man, Ichie Omaka who saw the rush of people each opting to be licensed to express his profound gratitude to God for the victory won, expressly summarize the meeting in a very concise speech saying yes, it is said that, all is not over until it is over. Therefore, let us end it here first before we miss the target or overreact to the victory granted to us by God. Let every man return to his tent for a good rest today and we shall fix a day to converge and happily celebrate this

God's given victory as we have, by the grace of God, recaptured our lost fatherland and are no longer slaves to any class, race, and creed in our fatherland.

However, I know that we cannot thank God enough for doing us this good but let all comments be reserved till the day of reckoning he greeted the people and they answered with a meticulous zeal. This declaration almost cut every other speech short irrespective of the rush of people and ended the partial celebration and people started dispersing the scene happily after the day and date were fixed. And it was designed to be on Eke market day when no man is practically expected to go to the farm but to relax at home and make merry for the successful completion of the four traditional market days known to the people. And they all prayed for the successful arrival of the D-day.

CHAPTER 11

A man cannot govern a nation if he cannot govern a city; he cannot govern a city if he cannot govern a family; he cannot govern a family if he cannot govern himself; and he cannot govern himself unless his passions are subject to reason and self-control.

The D-day successfully arrived. Many said it was just like a twinkling of an eye while some never believed it completed its circle. Although every arrangement for the grand occasion was previously completed that morning, they did some finishing touches, just as the people believed that "in the course of sounding drums, if there were no stylish incantation on it, it did not seem as if a drum was heard". However, this was not done without a purpose. It was done in waiting for the arrival of all the other villages and the whites who were also part and parcel of the grand occasion. Precisely speaking, at exactly eight o'clock that morning the playground was filled with people of different works of life including women and children seated at their quarters.

At this juncture, it was observed that all the elderly men of the village and the team of seven were seriously meeting at the compound of Hoary Onyedika where they unanimously appointed Hoary Ozurumba to open the august occasion with all that is required of an occasion such as this. Immediately this was settled, and the great Ikoro sound was heard. With this, the remaining people in the kingdom who were not at the playground were notified by the sound of Ikoro that the occasion was about to start. To this effect, all roads led to the playground and at exactly nine o'clock, the occasion started in earnest with a libation and opening prayer, and remarks by Hoary Ozurumba, who rose to the occasion perfectly well and conclusively reminded the entire kingdom that they were at the verge of success. And that, it is only their total support, cooperation, and commitment that shall help them fulfill their destiny.

To this end, Ichie Ichaka, quietly rose from where he was sitting, moved forward a little bit, almost to the Centre of the playground, and greeted the people craving their indulgence, and they answered. He started by appreciating the strong sense of patriotism exhibited by the team of seven which eventually completely changed their lives and story for the better. He summarily requested, according to directives, that the team of seven should please tell the entire kingdom what their mind was, about the survival of the kingdom. The leader and mouthpiece of the team happily rose to the occasion and as expected tactfully spoke the minds of all the individual members of the team in particular and the entire kingdom in general.

Frankly speaking, he tactfully and systematically took the entire people of the kingdom down memory lane and showcased their encounter with the whites. He tactfully x-rayed their ordeals with them from the first day they assumed power till power was forcefully taken away from them. That is, from the moment they launched their first ideological orientation which was coined in the brainwash education nicknamed or christened the two "Cs" which impliedly have "if you cannot convince them confuse them" as its working principle; till now they lost the grip of power, and finally said that they should or cannot continue to mortgage their children's future on the mountain of this confusion: "brainwash education". He continued, while did we struggle to live when we become a slave to destiny; when will we be free, when we die".

It was based on this premise that we accepted to fight this good fight because we believed that life is our right and so, we don't have to give up the fight. We fought for the answer to our collective prayers because we were able to manage our past and believed in the future. We had our collective dreams, although they say that" a "dream may seem amazing and without reason but it can explain reality". Today we are happy to say that "dreams are made of imagination and creativity". Therefore our success indicated that our dreams were valid because we were willing to roll up our sleeves, put in the work, and followed our passion. To this end, before we conclude our speech, we shall be very glad to hear from our brothers, the whites, for they are no longer our collective foes but friends and brothers.

In the same vein, Mac Allison, a grandson to the leader and mouthpiece of the white team at their arrival came on board and as the spirit of this renaissance was effective on him, greeted the people craving their indulgence, the people answered and there was a dead silence. The people were all ears eagerly waiting to hear him speak. However, in a laconic term, he said, "well my brothers, let me start by saying that it was not our fault because God will always make everything beautiful at its time. We are sincerely very sorry for talking and acting before thinking and reasoning. It is quite unfortunate or rather disheartening to note that what happened was a result of misinformation, miscalculation, and misconception of things. Because of our formal orientation, we had the hope that nothing destroys destiny like poverty; that, even good ambitions could be marred by poverty and to this effect, we introduced poverty to the system through our words and deeds and also force the people to feel inferior to us.

But we have genuinely realized that "if a man is feeling superior to someone who does not feel inferior to him, that such a man is walking on a very dangerous track, or is sitting on a gun powder. Of a truth, by the virtue of this team's work, we have been humbly made to know that the only good and excellent way of making and maintaining fame, better still, good fame, is not to raise heads in pride, genuflect before people and brag in the strength of wealth but to lower heads down and learn and demonstrate humility and honesty. It has also dawned on us what this team has demonstrated, that is, "don't maltreat any man, for one day, it will be your turn, for what goes round must come round".

It has buttressed the point which says "always be patient with God and time, for one day it will click your destiny". And with this scenario, we believed that there is nothing that we shall imagine to do under this gracious knowledge that shall be impossible. And so, we are not going to leave out the ethics of this renaissance. Whichever way or whatever means this great and heroic kingdom deems fit for the edification, survival, unity, and progress of the noble kingdom, we are solidly behind, in fact, we are happy partakers and partners of such programmes. He concluded his speech by greeting the people and they answered with meticulous zeal.

In this circumstance, this Godly declaration according to the people thrilled the entire people of the kingdom, and Ichie Ekumgbe, the noblest of the nobles, in the kingdom happily greeted the people, they happily answered and there was a dead silence. He continued, exclamatorily "humility thy name is success". I am particularly happy today because Mac Alison has spoken well for the first time in the history of our relationship with them, and gave a good flavor to the present occasion which impliedly means that we have passed the Ikamuagini syndrome characterized by measuring the worth of a man by what wealth he has wrongly or rightly acquired, not counting on his mental and physical quotient where every good thing is said to happen by accident and by the selfish desire of those at the corridor of power and in power.

I am also very happy that all our dreams come through because we dared to push them to a logical conclusion. I am equally happy that our circumstances were raw materials for these great miracles which have gone a long way to prove that, we are all special and peculiar in our ways. Yes, to a larger extent, the team has demonstrated and proved that "if one does not desire death, one will not succeed". No wonder our people always shout "monwu o" when they are in a difficult situation. Yes, we have realized that some people among us were good believers because they were careful sinners. However, I am also happy that we have come off that devil's philosophy inspired by greed for larger wealth, exploitation in the highest order, inordinate grabbing, coercion as a ready resort, and the hunt for power and more power over the known kingdom. Well, we still look onto the team to conclude their speech before we talk, because we have so much to say.

To this end, the leader and mouthpiece of the team immediately came on board again and greeted the people, the people answered and there was a dead silence. He continued, well, it is said that "the part of wisdom lies in changing those things that can be changed and accepting those things that cannot be changed". When one says, I am sorry, that does not mean that one is wrong, but just to maintain a good relationship and close ties that prevail among them. We are happy that man is a product of nature and nurture or what they call, learning begins in the cradle and ends in the grave; which means that learning never ends as long as man lives. We are also happy that, the "we...and them" syndrome which was only an imaginary story to manipulate or woo favour to enable one to achieve good and great fortunes for oneself, has ended.

However, let us not allow those centuries of greed and selfishness that robbed us or helped us achieve, influence our present relationship with one another to prove that it takes love to serve the people and that we should not wait until all our needs are completely met before we attend to people mercifully. Yes, to a greater extent, our success has shown that "anything a man's mind conceives of is possible" and life is more meaningful if only it is totally devoted and tactfully designed to provide succor to the suffering people and serve humanity in love. Yes, to know is to understand; and to understand means to change, and to change is to develop. Our success is like the hands of Africans that fertilized the womb of mother earth.

In summary, we have no intention of taking over the government of this great kingdom of our people. Our action was genuinely prompted by the emotion to stop that persistent man's inhumanity to man in the disguise of government and demonstrate the fact that, we should build an integrated state with a centralized administration and efficient personalities from what we considered a disorganized and rivalry–ravaged territory. Let us know that lies have short legs, and are only lies that make for illogical reasoning and argument; if any man pretends what he is not and gets to power, it is assumed he gets to power through back door and it is through the same back door he shall live because it is said: "that a lie will add to your troubles, subtract from your energy, multiplies your difficulties and divides your effectiveness."

Therefore, let whoever has the interest of the masses at heart and has the heart to serve the people in love come forth and seek an elective position to represent the people well at all levels of government. We need leaders that can transform our hell-like state into heaven–like state for us to live and have good and fulfilled lives. However, he who desires to lead has good ambition but lets his vision be guided by the will of the populace. Therefore, let our ambition be directed and guided by this vision. Let us know that our formal division was orchestrated by our artificial creation manipulated as the product of accidents of history. We should therefore eschew regional and ethnic or racial rancor and disunity to the best of our ability and knowledge but use our diversity to an enviable advantage by creating a viable, stable, strong political unit.

In this context, let us develop a philosophy of governance in which the masses will not be perceived as an exploitable group, and the leadership unaccountable to the people. Let us always apply loyalty, humility, honesty, and accountability, the quadrant stand that brings out the beauty in governance which abhors a class-conscious and capitalistic-oriented society in which the state was perceived basically as an instrument for exploiting the people and the resources of the society. Let us not continue to live in pretense or wait for prophets from any other place to come and interpret to us what this obnoxious and bedeviled "dive and rule policy" of our fathers has done to us because we are living witnesses to it. But we shall not also say that they were very wicked to us for adopting the policy of "mutually assured corruptive tendencies because it is said "no event no history. However, the vision awaits its time and we are happy today because the time is now.

Although it could be recalled that violence, corruption, arson, and brigandage were tactfully employed by the whites in their mad desires to continually rule over us, which manifested its harmful impact and effects in concrete ways by which it affected citizenship and the interest of persons and groups, who are usually easily neglected, manipulated and discriminated against because of their relative powerlessness vis-à-vis other persons and groups due to their handicap in numerical strength or social and biological deformities. But presently, for courtesy and leniency reasons, let our informing principle ever be the stability of our dear society.

Just as it is demonstrated by our divine and strange stream " Iyiekengbon" which comes from the same source but has two different colors, and part ways and defines its terms of operations. This also buttresses the saying that "when two equals meet, they define their terms of operations". Although it is said that, "the sheep that bleats too much makes itself a prey and is always the target of the predators, when it bleats, it will reveal its hidings and attracts the predators and should be the first to be cut off from the fold". I know and am persuaded that so many people may misinterpret or misunderstand what we are trying to say, but we expect every patriot to stand firm in the course of justice and righteousness. We did this under the working principle that," determination is often the first chapter in the book of excellence", and today we have finally arrived.

However, it is a well-known fact, that the whites having through various economic policies disarticulated our economy, ensured the continued economic dependence of our people through the grooming of a political class that has always served as conduit pipes for the imperialist exploitation of their fatherland. To a larger extent, this political class invariably becomes stooges in the hands of the exploiters against the exploited. In practice this meant that the inheritors of powers had the right to create and mobilize political resources without hindrances, to arrogantly appropriate to themselves all patronages in government jobs and appointments, to create networks of political clientage and use the bureaucracy, and the means of coercion to maintain themselves in office, to make themselves secure in their enjoyments of the lucrative rewards of politics. To maintain a foothold and strong grip on our dear society, decrees and edicts roll out in quick succession with the dumping of our existing code of conduct.

At this juncture, clannishness, nepotism, favoritism, and parochialism, automatically become the determining factor in who will be who in the government of our dear land. Thus, meritocracy was murdered in place of mediocrity, or simply put, meritocracy was tactfully sacrificed on the altar of mediocrity. It was correct to say that, the leadership of our land has always had the misfortune of falling into the hands of rapacious powers megalomaniacs, who owing to sheer incompetence and selfishness, were incapacitated by, or incapable of satisfying the yearnings and aspirations of our people. To this end, let us change our attitude and orientation about governance and administration. Let us know that governance is always beautified by loyalty, humility, honesty, and accountability.

The administration should not be seen as an end in itself as so many people think. But let it be seen as a series of communication channels that should transmit information, as the needs and aspirations of the people and ensure that these are reflected and respected in the way in which our society is governed. Equally these channels must be structured or so designed to transmit the aims and objectives of government to the people. In this circumstance, let us define our terms of operations, that is, the rights and duties of the governors and the governed to stop this cut-throat competition among us. However, I suggest that the two parties involved in this interest at stake should go and make consultations to evolve a more participatory and pragmatic system of the administration targeting our local areas to mobilize local resources for more effective rural development which shall combine socio-political, cultural and economic elements to institutionalize an acceptable and responsive strategy consistent with its own pace of development" I conclude my speech.

To be very frank, the people were happy about this well-prepared speech and as soon as he was done with it, one of the eldest men among them, Hoary Okamba, immediately came on board and greeted the people and they answered. He continued, my people, I am happy today for this gathering. I heartily appreciate this strong sense of patriotism and I happily thank our speaker for speaking boldly about the minds of the people of the kingdom. But before any other thing, I humbly wish to call on our brothers, the whites to briefly react to this speech. Then Mac Allison who is now the mouthpiece of the whites happily rose to the occasion and laconically summarized their notion about the issue at stake by saying that "all that the new kingdom has proposed for its success and progress is happily and heartily accepted by us.

To make our task easier for us, we count on the traditional system of government of our people where everyone was carried along, which exemplified inclusive governments, as all men were regarded to be created equal but with a different endowment, which is desired to be nourished and harnessed to the enrichment of all class or creed, notwithstanding the diversities of ethnic origin, culture, language or religion which may exist, which reflects the distinctive desire of the people to promote unity, foster loyalty, honesty, humility and responsibility and thereby give every citizen the sense of belonging and the right hand of fellowship to the society.

Let us organize a government that shall reflect the wishes, needs, and aspirations of the people as its vision which shall invariably reject in all ramifications the government of the whites which passed on to its wards the prejudices which had enabled them to think and act in the beliefs that the immediate past administration or relationship was a marriage of convenience between two incompatibles, where the whites looked down on the natives as uncivilized, pagans, indiscipline, rowdy and nakedly materialistic. And the natives returned this great contempt with a compliment, regarding the whites as imposters, feudalistic, conservatives, uneducated… and as the pliant tools of the imperial master. This ignited the struggle for economic advancement by individuals and communities and the fear of political and economic domination accentuated by the uneven development of disparate communities.

As we can see very vividly, our past government bequeathed to us an enduring legacy of mutual suspicion and contempt; and what remained constant and central to our father's system of government was its penchant for colouring relationships within our given communities. Where political contests were seen along lines of small group's interests, and individuals in government were perceived as good representatives of their groups. Impliedly this form of government or governance demanded therefore that, as individuals in their groups, members participated both in policy determination and in the distributions of values and/ or benefits. However, we know our problems and we cannot shy away from them or pretend as if we are not aware of them.

We are not waiting till a day is fixed for this. We need to thoughtfully present our recommendation based on these cardinal principles begging your approval: that government should comprise a grand coalition where all the main segments of our society are properly represented particularly as practiced in this noble kingdom in the time of old; that the decision- making process must be based on the mutual veto principle which means that the masses can veto any policy that does not conform with the traditional code of conduct; that it must not only recognize but also respect segments autonomy provided it is not against the overall interest of the kingdom. We rest our case.

As soon as he concluded his speech, ichie obichiri came on board expressing his happiness on the issue at stake. He happily thanked the last speaker and the mouthpiece of the other party for explicitly showcasing the expression that, everybody is tired of the immediate past system which invariably is beckoning on the old-time religion so to say, as the best system that could make its practitioners turn their hell-like communities into heavens and inhabit them joyfully. To this end, he recommended the next eke market day to be the grand finale and conclusion of their meeting which is expected to usher in a new era. It was happily carried and that impliedly marked the end of their meeting for that day. And people happily went back to their respective homes. However, within the remaining three days, to the fixed day and date, consultations were made. Although it was just to fulfill all righteousness since everyone was aware of their problem, compromises were also made, and finally, proposals were drawn up in wait for the arrival of the D-day.

However, the expected day and date successfully arrived. Before half past eight that morning, the playground was filled with people and without delay, Hoary Echendu was mandated to perform the libation and opening prayer for the ceremony which he did excellently well and declared the meeting or occasion open. After the cross-fertilization of ideas, they got to a point they called a turning point where they agreed to adopt themselves, and the growth and progress of the kingdom the following as their commandment. As a preamble, it reads thus; as it is said that "in the general course of human nature, a power over a man's subsistence amount to a power over his will", it was and in fact, is not surprising that those who were and are unrepresented in any public sphere felt and feel deprived.

Henceforth, the composition of our government or any of its agencies and the conduct of the affairs of this government or its agencies shall to the best of our knowledge be carried out or conducted in such manners as to recognize the diversity of the people within its area of authority and the need to promote a sense of belonging and loyalty among the people of our society. To actualize this, let us maintain a bottom-top relationship where people are allowed to plan their developmental goals and present them to the government for actualization as against the top-bottom relationship where the government imposes white elephant projects on the people in the name of development, which is, for the selfish interests of the actors in the helm of affairs in government, that existed before now to enable us to achieve the following objectives.

The principle aims of our government from this day shall be: 1. To make appropriate services and development activities responsive to local wishes and initiatives by developing or delegating them to local representative bodies; 2. To facilitate the exercise of democratic self-government closer to the local levels of our society as it was in the ancient times, and to encourage initiative and leadership potential; 3. To mobilize human and material resources through the involvement of members of the public in their local development; 4. To provide to the best of our ability and knowledge a two-way channel of communication between local communities and government; 5. There shall be the emergence of an enlightened leadership imbued with exquisite statesmanship, not only based on the formal education competence but also on the informal education competence, to direct the affairs of our society and to ensure the continued survival of peace, unity, stability, and integration of our kingdom without compromisingly capitalizing on, and fanning the embers of ethnic or racial differences among the various peoples of our kingdom, which we have abridged today, to win the support of the masses in their domains. For it is now our new task to invade the camp of those who shall by their words and deeds, ensconce the continued existence of such disparaging distinctions and inequalities among human beings. This shall also destroy the hob of doctored democracy based on, self-preservation, scarcity, criminal behavior, and the desire to secure material things occasioned by the writ of ownership whose fruits are fear, greed, worry, scarcity, competition, jealousy, envy, covetousness, strife, poverty, discrimination, racism, malice, and deceit.

To this end, the entire people of the new kingdom accepted all the provisions of the new commandment in good faith and assimilated it as their new code of conduct and guide in running the affairs of their government. They happily wined and dined till the sunset at about half past four O'clock in the evening and it was sealed with a libation and closing prayer by Hoary Ogombadiegwu.

CHAPTER 12
The surest way not to fail is
to determine to succeed.

However, the new kingdom has been without a leader throughout the renaissance period and now. To this effect, a solemn assembly was called and it was presided over by Ichie Ekeoma according to directives. In this circumstance, the playground looked intimidating as it was crowded with people and, for the first time since their struggle for freedom, both women and children were also in attendance. And this time, freedom is the true meaning of the word which is said to be complete when it addresses the issues of fear as freedom of conscience; want as freedom of economy; and protection as political freedom. Hoary Udechukwu performed the libation seen as the opening prayer and declared the meeting open.

Already everybody was aware of the agenda and the presiding officer decided to shift this burden to the womenfolk as a starting point or a takeoff ground for the discussion. And without delay, the mother of the womenfolk, Udu popularly addressed as Neayioha called on a few women to come over to the back of the women's stand or pavilion at the playground for a very brief discussion. It was done without delay and very briefly they met and handed everything over to the women leader, Ehihia Chukwu, Ochioha1, who perfectly rose to the occasion. As soon as they joined back the gathering and the women leader matched forward to the place specially prepared for women to seat and address the audience at the playground, Ichie Obinna greeted the people, craving their indulgence, according to tradition, for the womenfolk to open the parcel they tried at the back of their pavilion to all who were present at the gathering, the people happily answered and there was a dead silence.

Nne, Ehihichukwu, as she is popularly addressed came on board. And since the ground has already been cleared for her, she started, she started by saying, we, the entire womenfolk, are grateful that we were invited to this great occasion and were given the opportunity and license to contribute our quota to the issue at stake, that is, the proper building of our new kingdom. I stand here today on behalf of our womenfolk, even when she was sitting down because it is against their tradition for a mere woman to stand at the playground and address the audience, grateful to the God of heaven and to the gods of our land that our diversity opened up a new chapter and hope for us. I am also happy now that our collective dreams live on in our innermost man. I am equally happy that this great renaissance has spurred us into sharing not only an improbable love for ourselves but has also helped us share an abiding faith in the possibilities of this kingdom which we shall cherish to the end of the world.

However, we sincerely believe that in this new conducive and tolerant kingdom, nothing is going to be a barrier to our collective and individual successes because the new kingdom is established on the premise that in a generous kingdom like ours inhibited by a generous people, one does not have to be rich to achieve one's great potential. I stand here knowing that our individual story is part of the larger kingdom's story. That we individually owe a debt to all of those who came before us, and that, in no other kingdom on earth, is our story even possible. Today, we gather to, first of all, affirm the greatness of our kingdom, not because of the height of our physical or fiscal strength, the power of our able-bodied men of valor, or the size of our economy.

However, our pride is based on a very simple premise, summed up in a declaration made over ten centuries ago. We hold this truth to be self-evident, that all men are created equal and that, they are individually endowed by their creator with certain inalienable rights. Among these are life, liberty, and the pursuit of happiness.

This is the true genius of our dear new kingdom, a faith in the simple dreams of its people, orchestrated by the hope that we can tuck in our children at night and know that they are fed, clothed, and safe from harm. That we can say what we think; write what we think without hearing a sudden knock on the door. That we can have our idea and start our own business without paying a bribe or hiring somebody's son. That we can participate in the political process without fear of retribution, and that our votes will be counted and the true results announced. We, therefore, call for the reaffirming of our values and commitments, to hold them against hard reality, and see how we can measure up to the legacy of our forbearers and the promise of our future generations. And this shall be made possible under good leaders.

Precisely speaking, we are aware that, no people on earth expect the government to solve all their problems; but they sense deep in their bones, that with just a change in priorities, they can make sure that every child in their society shall have a decent shot at life and that the doors of opportunities remain open to all.

We are equally aware that, we can do better with this change. Our choice is that our new kingdom should change from kingship rule to leadership rule because our kings have been ruling us with iron hands. We have been helpless victims of this inhuman treatment in the name of kingship rule. The kings who have reigned over us, have always taken our sons and appointed them to their chariots and to be their horsemen and to run before their chariots. They have always appointed for themselves commanders of thousands and commanders of fifties and some to plough their grounds and to reap their harvest and to make their implements of war and the equipment of their chariot. They always take our dear daughters to be perfumers, cooks, and bakers. They take the best of fields and vineyards and olive orchards and give them to their servants. They take the tenth of our grains and our vineyards and give them to their officers and servants. They take our menservants and maidservant, and the best of our cattle and asses, and put them to their work. They take every good thing of our kingdom and we have been their slave. The government is corrupt because corrupt men make laws. We want a leadership rule where the wishes of a few opportunists will no longer be law, and where the leaders shall however understand the ideas of community faith and sacrifice because they are self-evident in their life or they have defined their lifestyle; shall also believe in our new kingdom where hard work is rewarded; shall equally believe in the constitutional freedom tactfully designed to make our new kingdom the envy of the whole wide world, and shall never sacrifice our basic liberties nor use faith as a wedge to divide us again. And this shall go a long way to determine our absolute faith in our new kingdom and its leader.

Consequently, we also suggest that we should change our formal name Agbozara, which capitalized on and fanned the embers of the ethnic differences, which amplified greed as the mother of waste, and raised the spin masters and negative ad peddlers who embraced the politics of anything goes as the father of exploitation to Orrah, which shall be capitalized on the principle of, or the fundamental belief that I am my brother's keeper which shall make our dear new kingdom work. This shall be our watchword and what shall direct us to pursue our dreams, yet, still come together as a single family. However, we shall rest our case here waiting for its approval by the men folk after complementing or garnishing it well as better bakers.

At this juncture, Ichie Mbadiwe came on board and enthusiastically greeted the people, the people answered with meticulous zeal and this officially ended the women leader's speech. Ichie Mbadiwe, in the same mood and spirit, thanked the entire women folk on behalf of the men for their good and seasoned contribution to the issue at stake. He continued, my people, shall we seek the services of a soothsayer to be convinced that we have eventually come to the end of the road of our problems? We are happy that "life without battle is life without victory".

Yes, our people say that "a woman who wants a child, does not sleep in her clothes". Yes just like what the slim bee said that "it does not mud and moist the baby when the weather is cool because the baby may get frozen and die but that it mud and moist the baby when the weather is hot to create a conducive atmosphere for the good growth and wellbeing of the baby. Yes, the cool weather is over, and here and now is the scorching heat of the sun. Who shall mud and moist us in this very hot weather to create a conducive atmosphere or enabling environment for our good growth and wellbeing. The diviner has divined and interpreted his divination, what else?

To this effect, Hoary Chukwuma came on board and cleared the air by greeting the people, they answered, and there was a dead silence. He continued, by first thanking the people for their open-mindedness to the issue at stake which he said was the only best way of proffering a long-lasting solution to any known problem of man. He openly told the people that our problem is ourselves. The system that was in operation in our kingdom was good enough to have helped us reach our collective and individual destinies. But, because of the nomenclature and definition of the term, we confused ourselves the more and made ourselves and the society exploitable materials to be damagingly exploited by the exploiters. What we termed marks of slavery were agents of civilization and modernization. And because of ideological orientations differences, what we termed hoodlums, God's sent, looters, etc. were not the actual meaning of the words in the actual sense.

Therefore, the first thing to do now if we want to get things right in our kingdom is to rebuild and redefine those terms we grossly abused because of our selfish inordinate ambitions and greed. It is only after this noble task that we shall be on the verge of success. We have indeed made wonderful commandments for ourselves but there must be reputable institutions to actually effect and efficiently implement the commandments to work out the expected miracles because everything in life or on earth goes in pairs. They are like the equation of two sides of which the two sides must balance before it could be called a complete equation.

To this end, they all understood what or where he was driving his points too. Immediately, it was carried. Few men in the name of the standing committee were chosen to direct the rehabilitation of all the destroyed churches and holy temples of the people. However, the people who saw these as their pet projects contributed willingly to the support of these projects. And, in no distant time, the projects were completed. This impliedly meant that the schools, churches, and holy temples of the people were built by the people and for the people. When this was concluded, the people joyfully fixed a day for the official adoption of their commandments and also for the celebration of their projects and the launching of a new name.

Eventually, the D-day came and every dick and Harry headed to the playground and happily seated at their various stands before seven O'clock in the morning. At exactly half past seven O'clock, the celebration started in earnest with a libation and opening prayer by Hoary Ejali, who perfectly did it well and officially declared the occasion open. The people jointly and happily commissioned the churches, schools, and holy temples of the people defined their modes and limits of operations, and assigned portfolios to them, which were based on the 4Cs of the 21st century millennium which are conciliation, cooperation, coordination and communication and launched their new name. To this end, the people happily celebrated the new dawn of development which lasted throughout the day.

They happily wined and dined together as one people with one purpose, future, and destiny, irrespective of their class or creed, color, nature or nurture, and this marked the beginning of corporate and harmonious living in the new kingdom. In the end, their philosophy of "mutually assured corruptive tendencies" was the change to "mutually assure corrective tendencies" where everybody was corrected in love which also assured the election of good and reputable leaders to the seat of power. And the occasion was concluded with a libation closing prayer by Hoary Echendu who did this perfectly well and in anticipation that the newly established institution shall carry out their legitimate duties without fear or favour. Consequent to the expectation and anticipation of the people, the institutions were up and doing in the exercise of their respective duties; and the composition of the institutions and the conduct of its affairs were carried out in such a manner as to ensure fair and equitable treatment for all the component communities and camps in the new kingdom. These good blends of ideas ushered them into conducting elections according to the ethics that establish them and after they studied all the institutions and people in the new kingdom and judged them worthy.

In this circumstance, the best of the people came out for the election. People who have the interest of the masses at heart and who knew the problem of the people because they were part and parcel of the system were genuinely elected. Not people who never lived in the society nor knew what the problems of the society were and who may continue to learn what the problem was till the end of their tenure without learning them let alone solving them; because it is widely said that "a man does not learn who to be left-handed at old age".

However, their previous selections in the name of elections were characterized by thuggery and violence because the people who came on board never knew what governance and election were all about because they were impostors in their fatherland and wanted to impose themselves and their style of governance on the people because of their exposure to the western world vices or perhaps their economic strength, were now peaceful and homely because they take the way of the native which recommended somebody for election on the grounds of the family background, nature and nurture and particularly personal contributions to the community that positively uplifted or aided sustainable development of the kingdom.

Consequently, this new leadership set the ball in motion, with the help of the people, they organized their health sector to give the same health coverage to everybody in the kingdom, be you a politician in the Headquarters or an ordinary man in the street. Their educational sector was also organized to incorporate every dick and Harry in the kingdom without any preferential treatment to any class or creed and did not provide or give any preference to an overseas certificate in terms of appointment or recruitment to public offices. They organized a special program for the people who have the grades, the drive, and will, but do not have the money to go to school. This special program was adopted from the special program, the leader and the mouthpiece of the team of seven organized which he called Orphans and Destitute Children Foundation. The new government also extended it to tertiary institutions because of the educational need of the people.

However, this special program was formally initiated and organized by the leader of the team of seven to sensitize, educate and encourage the populace, government and its agencies, and nongovernmental organizations as well on the need to contribute meaningfully and positively to the upliftment and development of these Orphans and destitute children educationally as a sure way of giving them the right hand of fellowship and appropriate sense of belonging. And, is also a way of checking the dreadful trend of poverty which had made life a bane and is still making life a bane for the greatest number of people. To this effect, from his latest findings, just as his assumption was based on this saying, "a man went into the bush with two knives to fetch firewood. The knife that was sharp as to have given him what he wanted to have no handle and the knife with handle was not sharp". O! What a paradox.

In this circumstance, he observed that some of the privileged children were spoilt in loosed living in the name of adequately providing everything they needed which resulted in the waywardness of these children in the future and a low pace of both human and community development. Accordingly, it was very disheartening to note that the less privileged children who had the drive and the will to be educated were abandoned to their fate and were rather exposed to all manners of child abuse. Based on the above background, for a start, he carefully and systematically selected up to two hundred and fifty-two children, with the help of good-spirited and honest people of these sub-communities that made up their camp according to their population and as his financial strength could cover or carry. They were arranged as stated below: formal Orra Community which is now the political headquarters had twenty children from primary 4, 5, and 6; twenty students from Jss1, 2, and 3; sixteen children who were above primary school age but have not started because their parents had no money; sixteen children who were above secondary school age but have not started for the same as stated above.

In Amikpo Community, ten children from primary 4, 5, and 6; ten students from Jss1, 2, and 3; eight children who were above primary age but have not started because of the same reason stated above; and eight children who were above secondary school age but have not started because of the same reason as stated above were selected. Amorie community; Imama Community; Amozarah Community; and Agba Community had the same proportion as Amikpo Community because they were almost the same in population but not in land mass.

Consequent upon this, each child so selected had a file jacket which contained all the particulars of the child and the account number. Every relief package or bursary is given to each child in terms of wear, handiwork, books, and food was filed in the child's file jacket. And each child was designed to have a savings account with an initial deposit of ₦2,000.00 only with a monthly fixed deposit of ₦ 200.00 only. Structurally speaking this was done in cognizance of the fact that he knew or understood the psychological effect of improper dressing, wearing worn-out clothes to school, inability to pay for handwork and buy books, and an imbalanced diet on the part of a child. And so, the program was designed to emancipate these children from this ugly mental torture.

However, by his calculation, he anticipated that at the end of their primary and post-primary education, each child shall be richer by at least ₦30,000.00, and ₦26,000.00 for primary and post-primary children respectively to fall back on, which may sometimes sustain them within the time they may be unemployed or enable them to have something doing or facilitate their employment processes without being a burden to their poor parents or become a nuisance to the public. This may also save the entire society, by his calculation, from the ravaging scourge of armed robbery and reduce the rate of juvenile delinquencies or reclaim the young people in all communities or camps across the kingdom from violence and despair. Another grant foundation was founded in partnership with the government of the day whose motto was, conquer fear, conquer all; vision: take care of your future; mission: bring back the indignity of man; purpose: provide a grant to the actual poor.

And so, based on the success of this system, and other such good programs of the kingdom, they enjoyed peace and stability in the highest order, had respect and love for one another, flourish in progress as they worked with one mind, allowing every star to shine without being eclipsed by any other star taking cognizance of the fact that nobody knows the star that may or could lead the entire kingdom to where good things were, just as a star led the three wise men to where baby Jesus was born, and their unity and success were preached all over the world till this day.